D0835593

700037545047

THE WEEKEND

THE WEEKEND

Bernhard Schlink

TRANSLATED FROM THE GERMAN BY
Shaun Whiteside

Weidenfeld & Nicolson
LONDON

First published in Great Britain in 2010 by Weidenfeld & Nicolson,
An imprint of The Orion Publishing Group Ltd
Orion House, 5 Upper Saint Martin's Lane
London WC2H 9EA

An Hachette UK Company

1 3 5 7 9 10 8 6 4 2

Originally published in German as *Das Wochenende*
by Diogenes Verlag AG, Zürich, in 2008

Grateful acknowledgement is made to Walter Popp for his
consultation on the translation.

A CIP catalogue record for this book is
available from the British Library.

ISBN 978 0 297 86317 5

Printed in Great Britain by Clays Ltd, St Ives plc

The Orion Publishing Group's policy is to use papers that are natural, renewable
and recyclable products and made from wood grown in sustainable forests.
The logging and manufacturing processes are expected to conform to the
environmental regulations of the country of origin.

www.orionbooks.co.uk

Friday

She got there just before seven. She'd expected to make more headway and arrive sooner by traveling in the early morning. When she hit more road construction, and yet more, she grew nervous. Would he walk through the gate, look out for her in vain, his first reaction one of disappointment, of discouragement? The sun rose in the rearview mirror—she would rather have been driving toward it than away from it, even if it had dazzled her.

She parked where she had always parked and walked the short path to the gate as slowly as she had always walked. Everything to do with her own life she cleared from her mind, to make room for him. He always had a firm place in her mind; not an hour passed without her wondering what he was doing right now, how he was getting on. But each time she met him, he alone existed for her. Now that his life was no longer in suspended animation, now that it was starting to move once more, he needed her full attention.

The old sandstone building stood in the sun. As so often before, she was strangely moved that a building should serve such an ugly purpose and at the same time be so beautiful: the walls covered with Virginia creeper, field and forest green in spring and summer, yellow and red in autumn, the small towers on the corners and the

large one in the middle, its windows like those of a
church, the heavy gate, forbidding, as if it wished not to
shut the inhabitants in but to shut their enemies out. She
looked at the clock. The people in there liked to keep
you waiting. She had often applied in vain for a two-
hour visit, and after the hour granted, was simply not
collected but went on sitting with him for another half
hour, three quarters of an hour, without really being
with him any longer.

But when the bells of the nearby church began to
strike seven, the gate opened and he stepped out and
blinked into the sun. She crossed the street and
embraced him. She embraced him before he could set
down his two big bags, and he stood in her embrace
without returning it. "At last," she said, "at last."

"Let me drive," he said as they stood by the car,
"I've dreamed of it so many times."

"Are you sure? Cars have got faster, the traffic's
heavier."

He insisted, and kept driving even when the sweat
stood out on his brow. She sat tensely next to him and
said nothing when he made mistakes turning in the city
and overtaking on the autobahn. Until they passed a
sign for a service station and she said, "I need some
breakfast, I've been up for five hours."

She had visited him in prison every two weeks. But
when he walked along the counter with her, filled his
tray, stood at the till, came back from the toilet and sat
down facing her, she felt as if she were seeing him for
the first time in ages. She saw how old he had become,
older than she had noticed or admitted during her visits.

At first glance he was still a handsome man, tall, square face, bright green eyes, thick salt-and-pepper hair. But his poor posture emphasized his little paunch, which didn't match his thin arms and legs, his gait was slow, his face gray, and the wrinkles that crisscrossed his forehead, and were steep and long in his cheeks, indicated not concentration so much as a vague sense of strain. And when he spoke—she was startled by the awkwardness and hesitancy with which he responded to what she said, and the random, jittery hand movements with which he emphasized his words. How could she have failed to notice that on her visits? What else was happening, in him and to him, that she had also failed to notice?

"Are we going to your place?"

"We're going to the country for the weekend. Margarete and I have bought a house in Brandenburg, run-down, no heating, no electricity, and the only water comes from the pump outside, but it's got a big, old park. It's gorgeous now, in the summer."

"How do you cook?"

She laughed. "Are you interested in that? With great fat red gas canisters. I've ordered an extra two for the weekend; I've invited our old friends."

She'd hoped he'd be pleased. But he showed no pleasure. He only asked: "Who?"

She had thought long and hard. Which old friends would do him good, which would only make him embarrassed or reserved? He needs to be among people, she thought. And more than that, he needs help. Who will he get that from, if not his old friends? Finally she decided that the ones who were pleased she had called, the ones who wanted to come, were also the right ones. In some of those who made excuses she sensed honest regret; they would have liked to be there if they'd known about it earlier, if they hadn't already made other plans. But what was she to do? His release had come as a surprise.

"Henner, Ilse, Ulrich with his second wife and their daughter, Karin with her husband, Andreas, of course. With you, Margarete and me that's eleven."

"Marko Hahn?"

"Who?"

"You know the one—for a long time he just wrote to me. He visited me for the first time four years ago and he's been a regular visitor ever since. Apart from you he's . . ."

"You mean that lunatic who nearly cost you your reprieve?"

"He only did as I asked. I wrote the welcoming speech, I knew who the addressees were, what the occasion was. You have nothing to reproach him for."

"You couldn't have known what you were doing. He did know, and he didn't try to stop you, he just rode on into it. He uses you." She was as furious now as she had been that morning, reading in the paper that he had written the welcoming address for an obscure left-wing conference on the theme of violence. His actions, the paper said, had revealed his incapacity for insight and remorse—such a person didn't deserve to be reprieved.

"I'll give him a call and invite him." He got up, looked for and found some coins in his trouser pocket and walked to the phone. She got up too, was about to run after him and stop him, then sat back down again. When she saw he didn't know where to take the conversation, she got back up, walked over to him, took the receiver and described the route to her house. He put his arm around her, and it felt so good that she was reconciled.

When they drove on, she was at the wheel. After a while he asked, "Why didn't you invite my son?"

"I called him and he just put the phone down. Then I wrote him a letter." She shrugged. "I knew you'd want him to be there. I also knew he wouldn't come. He decided against you a long time ago."

"That wasn't him. That was them."

"What difference does it make? He's become the person they brought up."

Two

Henner didn't know what to make of the weekend they were about to spend together, and what he should expect from it: from meeting Jörg again, along with Christiane and his other old friends. When Christiane's call had come, he had said yes right away. Because he had heard a plea in her voice? Because a friendship formed in youth can claim a lifelong loyalty? Out of curiosity?

He turned up early. He had seen on the map that Christiane's house bordered a nature reserve, and before he saw her again he wanted to take a walk. To walk, get some air in his lungs, switch off. Just that Wednesday he had returned from a conference in New York to the tyranny of his crowded desk and his crowded schedule.

He was surprised to see how grand the estate was: stone wall, iron gate, tall oak tree in front of the house and expanse of parkland behind it, the house itself a baronial mansion several centuries old. Everything was dilapidated. The roof was covered with rusty corrugated iron, the plaster on the exterior was flaky and mildewed and the meadow overlooked by the terrace at the back was overgrown with weeds and scrub. But the windows were new, there was fresh gravel out in front, wooden beer-garden furniture on the terrace, a table and four chairs already up, more tables and chairs still folded and the paths leading to the park had been cleared of weeds.

Henner took one of the paths and was plunged into a quiet, green forest world; above him he saw not sky, but sunlit foliage, and on either side of the grassy path the thicket of branches and bushes seemed impenetrable. For a while a bird had hopped or flown ahead of him. Henner understood that the many twists and turns in the path were there because the architect had wanted to make the park seem enormous. Even so, he felt as if he were in an enchanted wood, as if he had been cursed never to find his way back out. Just when he was starting to think he really wouldn't find his way back out, the forest world came to an end and he was standing by a wide stream; there were fields on the opposite bank and in the distance a village with a church tower and grain silos. Everything was still very quiet.

Then he saw a woman sitting on a bench downstream. She had been writing, had lowered her notebook and pencil to her lap and was looking at him. He walked over to her. A little gray mouse, he thought, nondescript, gauche, insecure. She looked back at him. "So you don't recognize me?"

"Ilse!" So often he found himself facing a familiar person and just couldn't think of his or her name—he was pleased that he had immediately put a name to a face that he had almost failed to recognize. When he had last seen Ilse sometime in the seventies, she had been a pretty young woman, her nose and chin slightly pointed, her mouth slightly severe, her back always slightly bent so that her big breasts didn't draw attention, but she glowed, a pale-skinned, blue-eyed blonde. Now Henner could no longer see that glow, although she was reacting with a friendly smile to their meeting, to his recognition of her. He felt uncomfortable, as if the fact that she had not become what she had promised to be and remain were somehow embarrassing. "How are you?"

"I've taken some time off. Three English classes— my friend stepped in for me, and I'm sure she'll do a good job, but I'd feel better if she called me or if I had some way of contacting her." She looked at him as if he might be able to help her. "I've never done that before: just take time off."

"Where do you teach?"

"I stayed. When the rest of you left, I finished my teaching diploma, got my first job and then my second, at my old school. I still have it: German, English, art." As if she wanted to get it out of the way, she went on: "I have no children. I never married. I have two cats and an apartment of my own on the mountain with a view of the plain. I like teaching. Sometimes I think thirty years is enough, but everybody thinks that about their job. And there isn't much longer to go."

Henner waited for a question in return: And how are you? When it didn't come, he asked another question: "Did you stay in contact with Jörg and Christiane?"

She shook her head. "I bumped into Christiane a few years ago at the Frankfurt station—the railway timetable was in chaos because of the snow, and we were waiting for our connecting trains. Since then we've talked on the phone from time to time. She said I should write to Jörg, but for a long time I didn't dare to.

II

I did when he made his application. 'I'm not asking for mercy. I fought against this state, and it has fought against me, and we owe each other nothing. We owe loyalty only to a single cause.' You remember? The announcement that he'd applied for a reprieve was so filled with pride—all of a sudden Jörg was once again the boy I'd known. The boy I'd fallen in love with." She smiled. "He didn't notice at the time, and neither did the rest of you. You were all . . . I was always afraid of you. Because you knew so precisely what was right and what was wrong and what needed to be done, because you were so resolute, unconditional, unbending, fearless. Everything was easy for you, and I was ashamed that it was hard for me and I didn't know a thing about capital and the state and the ruling class, and when you talked about pigs . . ." She shook her head again, lost in her past shame and fear. "And I had to graduate quickly and start earning money, and you had all the money and all the time in the world, and your fathers—Jörg and Christiane's was a professor, yours was a lawyer, Ulrich's was a dentist with a big practice and Karin's was a vicar. My father had lost his little farm in Silesia, which had hardly fed him but which had belonged to him, and was working in a dairy. 'Our milkmaid,' you sometimes called me, and I think it was meant nicely, but I didn't fit in with the rest of you, and it was more that you sort of put up with me, and if I'd disappeared . . ."

Henner tried to find memories that matched Ilse's. Had he presented himself as someone who knew everything quite precisely and had all the time in the world? Had he talked about policemen, judges or politicians as pigs? Had he called Ilse "our milkmaid"? It was all far away. He remembered the atmosphere on those nights when they had talked till dawn over too many cigarettes and too much cheap red wine, the constant feeling of searching for something, of needing to find the correct analysis, the correct action, the excitement of shared plans and preparations, and the sheer intensity of it, the intense enjoyment of their own strength, when the lecture hall belonged to them, or the street did. But there was nothing in his memories of what they had talked about and what they had actually been searching for and why lecture halls and streets needed to be conquered, and certainly nothing of how it had been for Ilse. Had she fetched them their cigarettes and made coffee for them? She was an art teacher—had she made posters for them? "I'm glad you took care of Jörg. I visited him when he was convicted, and couldn't get a sensible sentence out of him. That was it—until I got that call from Christiane a week ago. Has he changed a lot?"

"Oh, I didn't visit him—I just wrote to him. He never invited me." She looked at him quizzically. He didn't know whether it was his lack of interest in Jörg over all those years that she didn't understand, or his present interest in how Jörg might have changed. "We'll soon see, won't we?"

Three

When Henner had gone, Ilse opened her notebook and read what she had written.

> *The funeral took place on a warm, sunny day. It was a day when one could have driven to a lake, swum, spread out a blanket, unpacked red wine, bread and cheese, eaten and drunk, gazed into the sky and let one's thoughts drift with the clouds. Not a day for grieving, not a day for being dead.*
>
> > *The mourners were waiting outside the church. They greeted one another, recognized one another or introduced themselves; they were embarrassed. Every word was wrong. The expressions of sympathy were strained, the shared memories pallid, and if someone asked why, the question was helplessly and irritably dismissed. Every word was wrong, because Jan's death was wrong. He shouldn't have killed himself, shouldn't have left his three children orphans and his wife a widow. If you can't bear to be with your wife and children anymore, you get divorced. Killing yourself, sneaking off and leaving your wife and children with feelings of guilt—it's not the proper thing to do.*
> >
> > > *That's what one of the group of old friends says. Another one shakes his head. "Jan married Ulla*

when she got pregnant, after the first child he let her have the twins so she wouldn't notice that he didn't love her, he gave up university and became a lawyer so that Ulla and the children could live in clover, he paid for everything at home so that Ulla could finish her studies—all because it's the proper thing to do. How long can you keep that up? Deny yourself, because it's the proper thing to do? And if that's what you do— aren't you then as good as dead anyway?" A third one stops him. "Here comes Ulla."

In the church Jan's father speaks. He talks about the incomprehensibility of what has happened: beloved Jan suddenly disappearing and a few days later found dead in Normandy poisoned by the exhaust fumes that he had piped into his car, the car parked with a view of the sea, near a place where he had once been particularly happy years before. He speaks of the incomprehensible violence of the depressive impulse that not only drove Jan to flee his family and his job, but drove him to his death. He is the white-haired head of a family of many children and grandchildren, a retired vicar, and he speaks of the depressive impulse with an authority that impresses even the friends who can't remember ever having known Jan to be depressive. Do they know better than his father?

Ilse saw the funeral clearly again. It was the last time she had seen the friends with whom she was about to spend the weekend. Jörg had disappeared shortly after- ward. At the funeral he had had nothing but contempt for Jan; you don't throw your life away over bourgeois idiocies when there's a great struggle that it could be used for. Christiane had sensed what was happening to Jörg, hovered around him and confirmed his contemptuous and revolutionary views as if she wanted to show him that he had a place in the world with them, and that he mustn't disappear on their account. Soon afterward the others also scattered to the four winds. In a way Jörg had done what all the others had also needed to do at the time: he had determined the course of his life.

But it wasn't the impending meeting with these friends that had made her recall the funeral. It had only prompted her to start writing. She had bought a big, fat hardback notebook and a green mechanical pencil with a long lead of the kind that, it was explained to her—and she was pleased by the fact—was used by architects. On Thursday she had set off after school and come here by train and bus and taxi in order, the next morning, to do in a strange place what she didn't dare do at home: write.

No, her preoccupation with the funeral had begun years before. She had read about a play that contained an image from September 11 that she couldn't get out of her mind. Not the image of the airplanes flying into the towers, not the image of the towers smoking, or of them collapsing, not the image of the people covered in ash. What she couldn't get out of her mind was the image of the falling bodies, some singly, some in pairs, almost touching one another or even holding hands. It was always before her eyes.

Ilse had read everything she could find. That estimates of the number of falling bodies varied between fifty and two hundred. That lots of people jumped, but that some had fled to the windows and, when the panes exploded, had been forced out by other people jumping out or sucked out by the draft of air. That of those who jumped, some had decided to jump because of their hopeless situation, while the rest were simply driven out by the unbearable heat. That the heat rose to above 550 degrees Centigrade and reached the people before the flames reached them. That the drop was some four hundred meters, and the fall lasted up to ten seconds. That the pictures of the falling bodies were too blurred for faces to be made out. That relatives sometimes thought they could recognize a falling body by its clothes, and were partly comforted, partly terrified by that. And that among the dead, those who had fallen could not be identified.

But no information moved her as much as the pictures did. The falling bodies, always with both arms and often with all their limbs outstretched. Perhaps rather than the individual photographs that she found in books she might also have searched for film clips and seen the bodies actually falling, flailing, twisting, but she was scared to do so. Some of the falling bodies looked in the photographs as if they were floating to the ground or even flying away. Ilse hoped and doubted. Could someone do that? In such a situation could someone jump and then float, fly, even if it was only for the last ten seconds? Could he enjoy those ten seconds, which would end with a sudden and painless death, with all the delight that we are capable of bringing to the enjoyment of life?

In the play a man was supposed to be sitting in his office in one of the Twin Towers on the morning of September 11, but he was late for work and realized he had the opportunity to be dead to everybody, could sneak away from his old life and start a new one. Ilse hadn't seen or read the play. In her imagination the man had seen the pictures of the falling, floating, flying bodies and that had given him the idea of wanting to fly away—that made sense to her, that was enough. And it filled her imagination and it summoned up the memory of Jan's funeral and with it the question of whether he had actually killed himself or whether he had abandoned his old life to start a new one. Everything that had preoccupied both her and Ulla in the year after Jan's death came back to her, from the funeral to the mysterious phone call, the strange clothes, the missing files, the autopsy report.

Four

When Henner came back to the house after taking a wide sweep across the fields, another car was parked outside the gate, a big silver Mercedes with a Hamburg license plate. The door to the house was open. Henner went in, and when his eyes had grown accustomed to the half-light, he saw a staircase on the left leading up to the next floor and a hallway that ended in doors on each side. Both stairs and hallway were supported by a metal scaffolding. Again the plaster was flaking from the walls, and many of the natural stone slabs in the floor had been replaced by blobs of cement. But everything was clean, and opposite the front door a big vase of brightly colored tulips stood on an old table.

Upstairs a door opened and, closed, and for a moment talking and laughter rang out from the room behind it. Henner looked up. With slow, heavy steps, her left hand resting on the banister, a woman came down the stairs. As if she had pains in her left hip or her left leg, Henner thought, and she was too fat. He put her at fifty, a few years younger than himself. She was too young to be suffering from arthritis. Had she had an accident?

"Have you just got here too?" He nodded toward where the Mercedes was parked in front of the house.

She laughed. "No." She too gave a brief nod in the

direction of the Mercedes. "That's Ulrich with his wife and daughter. I'm Margarete, Christiane's friend, and I belong here. I have to get back to the kitchen—will you come and help me?"

For the next hour he stood in the kitchen, peeled potatoes and cut them into slices, diced pickled gherkins, chopped chives and received instructions about what needed to be stirred into the salad dressing. "Shaken, not stirred"—he attempted a joke. Margarete's ease, composure, cheerfulness irritated him. It was the cheerfulness of simple folk, the composure of those lucky devils who are at home in the world without having to work for it—Henner didn't like either quality. Her physical aura irritated him too. It was an erotic aura that he found doubly incomprehensible; he didn't like fat women—his girlfriends were always as slim as models—and Margarete, who wasn't at all impressed by his charm, was possibly more than just a friend of Christiane's. Possibly, too, she knew more about him than a girlfriend knows. If he thought back to that one night years ago with Christiane, he felt used again, and hurt. At the same time Christiane's behavior back then still seemed so strange that he felt once more that there was something he hadn't understood, and the fear that he had failed. Was that what had brought him here? Had Christiane's call aroused the desire to know at last what had really happened back then?

"Would you like to try the punch?" She held a glass out to him and he could tell that she'd asked him once already. He blushed.

"Sorry." He took the glass. "Love to." It was punch

with white peaches, and the taste reminded him of his childhood, when there had been no yellow peaches, only white ones, and how his mother had planted two peach trees in the garden. He gave the empty glass back to Margarete. "I've finished the potato salad. Is there anything else I can do? Do you know where I'm sleeping?"

"I'll show you."

But Ulrich, his wife and daughter were coming toward them down the stairs. Little Ulrich with his tall wife and tall daughter. Henner let himself be greeted and hugged and taken out onto the terrace. Ulrich's bumptious, cloddish qualities were too much for him, as they had been years before, and he was unsettled by the way his wife liked to throw her head back when she laughed, and the way his daughter posed around the place, bored and provocative, with her long legs crossed, short skirt, tight top and sulky mouth.

"No electricity—we'll have to go sit in my car if we want to hear the President. It said on the news a moment ago that he's going to deliver his speech in Berlin Cathedral, and I'm willing to bet that he'll announce Jörg's pardon. Very nice, I'd have to say, very nice of him to do it, when Jörg is already out, when he's been able to find a spot where the reporters and the cameras can't find him." Ulrich looked around. "Not a bad spot, not a bad spot. But he can't hide out here forever. Do you know what his plans are? They take on people like him in the arts, working as stagehands or doing lighting or proofreading. I'd be happy for him to start in one of my dental labs, but that wouldn't be chic enough for him. No offense, but because I gave up my studies to become a dental technician, you guys have always despised me a bit."

Again, Henner had to struggle to remember. When they'd gone to demonstrations Ulrich had always been there, and when there had been a butyric acid attack on a politician he had been the one who got hold of the harmless but foul-smelling liquid. Despised him? In those days they wouldn't have despised a working Ulrich, they would have admired him. He told Ulrich that.

"Really, forget about it. I sometimes read your pieces—excellent stuff. And the papers you write for—*Stern, Der Spiegel, Süddeutsche Zeitung*—prime addresses. The intellectual side of things has never really been my scene; I mean, I follow it, but I stay out of it myself. But where business is concerned—I think with my dental labs I'm way ahead of you intellectuals. So everyone does his own thing, you, me and Jörg. That's what I said to myself when I got Christiane's call. Everyone does his own thing, I said to myself. Jörg screwed up, he paid for it and now he's got to get his life back in order. It isn't going to be easy for him. In the old days he didn't know how to work and get on with people and live in peace with the world—why should he be able to do it now? I don't reckon it's something you learn in jail—what do you think?"

Henner didn't get a chance to say that he didn't know. Karin and her husband came out of the house onto the terrace. Henner was glad to see a familiar face, and glad that he immediately remembered her name. She had been a vicar, and had become the bishop of a little diocese, and he had interviewed her a few years before about the church and politics, and in the past year he had appeared with her on a talk show. On both occasions he had been glad to note that it had been no coincidence that he had liked her at university. Her soundness pleased him, so he forgave her for the marked gentleness and solemnity in her voice and her speech. Vicars just become unctuous, as journalists become boastful. And even though you can never tell with vicars how much their friendliness is due to their job and how much it is based on genuine sympathy, Henner had a sense that she was pleased to see him again too. Her husband, Eberhard, the retired curator of a South German museum, was much older than his wife, and the loving attention with which he fetched a shawl and put it around her shoulders when it grew cooler, and the affection with which she thanked him, made Henner think that this love fulfilled the longing of a daughter and a father. The husband saw through the arrangement of people around the table before sitting down, placing his chair between Ulrich's wife, Ingeborg, and daughter, Dorle, and managing to draw them both into conversation, even raising the occasional peal of merry laughter from that bored, provocative, sulky mouth.

As Margarete walked Andreas onto the terrace, she announced that Jörg and Christiane had called and would be arriving in half an hour. At six o'clock there would be an aperitif on the terrace, and at seven o'clock dinner in the drawing room—if anyone wanted to stretch their legs before evening, now was the time. She would summon them with the bell just before six.

While the others stayed where they were, Henner got up. Andreas wasn't one of the old friends who had met at school or in the first few terms at university. He had been Jörg's defense counsel until giving up his mandate because Jörg and the other defendants had wanted to exploit him politically. He became his lawyer again when Jörg requested his support in his bid for an early release a few years previously. Henner had met him before too. If the afternoon's choreography was designed to allow the guests to meet before everything started revolving around Jörg, Henner could take his leave. And besides, he didn't know how he would be able to bear so many people for so many hours in such a small space.

Once again he took a wide arc around the fields. He walked slowly, in a gangly fashion, taking long strides and swinging his arms. He hadn't phoned his mother from New York—he hadn't even phoned her since he'd got back, and he felt guilty even though he knew that she wouldn't remember when he had phoned her last. He hated the ritual of phone calls in which his mother repeatedly demanded that he speak up, before finally giving up and putting down the receiver, so that in the end nothing had been said. He hated the ritual of the visits that his mother looked forward to, but which always disappointed her because she sensed his distance. But without that distance he couldn't have borne her and her illnesses, laments and accusations. His hand played with the phone in his jacket pocket, snapped it open and shut, open and shut. No, he wouldn't call until Sunday.

Just before six he came back to the house, from the side this time, across an orchard, past a greenhouse with a big woodpile beneath a low roof. At the side, too, there was an oak tree, small and bent after being struck by lightning, and a door to the house. As he stood under the tree and looked into the evening, Margarete opened the door, wiped her hands on her apron, leaned against the door frame and looked into the evening, as he was doing. A bell hung beside the door; in a moment Margarete would step away from the door frame, grab the short bell pull with her powerful, bare arms and ring the bell. Henner didn't know she'd noticed him until she asked him, just loudly enough for him to hear her across the distance between them, and without turning around to him: "Do you hear the blackbirds' duet?" He hadn't paid any attention; now he heard it. The evening, the blackbirds, Margarete in the doorway—Henner didn't know why, but he was close to tears.

Five

Ilse didn't hear the bell. She was sitting in her room, on the other side of the house, writing. The room was furnished with a camp bed, chair and table; on the table there were a jug and basin, a candle, a box of matches and a bunch of tulips. It was a corner room; from one window Ilse could look out onto the oak and behind it a barn, from the other onto the gate.

> *The day after the funeral two lawyers came from Jan's office to Ulla's house. It was afternoon; the children were waiting for dinner and running noisily through the house. The older lawyer introduced himself as the senior partner of the office, the younger as the colleague with whom Jan had worked particularly closely. Ulla recognized them both; they had paid their respects to her the previous day, and the younger man had once come to pick up Jan.*
>
> *"We spoke on the phone to the police in France. They didn't find the files your husband had just been working on in the car. Would you forgive us for asking whether the files are here?"*
>
> *"I'll have a look this evening."*
>
> *But that wasn't enough for the two men. It was a matter of urgency, said the younger man, but she mustn't go to any trouble, he knew the way, and he*

slipped past her and up the stairs. The older man asked her to bear with them and apologized and followed the younger man into Jan's study. Ulla wanted to go with them, but the twins were arguing, and the water was boiling. She forgot the lawyers. When she was sitting with the children at the dinner table, they emerged from Jan's study. Their arms were full of files, but no, they hadn't found the files for which they had come.

The phone call came the same evening. Ulla had put the children to bed and was sitting at the kitchen table, too exhausted to feel pain or grief. She just wanted to lie down and go to sleep, and not wake up again in a new normality until several weeks or months had passed. But she didn't have the strength to get up, climb the stairs to the bedroom and go to bed. And she answered the telephone only because it was mounted on the wall in such a way that she could pick up the receiver without getting to her feet. "Hello?"

No one answered. Then she heard the caller breathing, and it was his breath. She knew it very well, and she loved it, loved the pauses in their telephone conversations, when he was wordlessly close to her with his breath. "Jan," she said. "Jan, say something—where are you, what's going on?" But he didn't speak, and when after anxious waiting she said, "Jan!" again, he hung up.

She sat there as if anesthetized. She was sure she hadn't been mistaken. She was sure that she must have been mistaken. She had seen Jan lying in the coffin. Jan.

Two days later she received the autopsy report in the mail. Name, sex, date and place of birth, body measurements and physical features—she had problems with the French text only when the incisions and results were described. She fetched the dictionary and went to work, even though the account of each incision caused her pain. When she was finished, she read the whole text all the way through again. Only now did she think of the sweatshirt and jeans in which Jan had lain on the table in front of the doctor. He had driven to the office in his suit that day. And, the police had written in their report, he had been found in his suit in the car.

She went to their shared wardrobe. She knew his clothes, even his jeans, his T-shirts and sweatshirts. Nothing was missing—as if it mattered. She called the undertakers. Somewhat surprised, they told her that her husband, when he was brought back from France, had been wearing a crumpled suit. She had been asked if she wanted to have it—didn't she remember?

The same evening, when the children were asleep, Ulla rang Ilse. She couldn't bear being on her own anymore. Ilse came dutifully. She and Ulla were not close friends. But if Ulla was lonely and desperate enough to seek comfort from her, then Ilse would give what she could.

Ulla didn't want comfort. She had put a suit of armor around her pain. She wanted to fight. She was sure that an ugly game was being played, and she wasn't prepared to take it. Who was behind it? What

had they done with Jan? Had they abducted him?
Abducted and murdered him?

Ilse set down her notepad and pen and looked out of
the window. She and Ulla had been in a frenzied state
back then. All the things they had tried! The search for
the client with whom Jan had been most involved over
the previous weeks, and about whom he had occasion-
ally dropped dark hints. The shadowing of her by the
office, which refused to let go because of the files. The
trip to Normandy. No hypothesis was too absurd, no
speculation too abstruse. Until after a year the giddiness
had run out and with it their friendship. Ulla was
insulted because Ilse didn't agree with her that Jan had,
as the result of some foul play by his office or a client,
been driven to suicide or abducted and murdered, but
insisted that he had only faked his death and was now
living a new life. They still met, still called each other,
but the intervals between meeting and calling grew
longer, and in the end each was relieved that the other
stopped.

Ilse understood why Ulla had fallen into that
frenzy. It enabled her to sail swiftly across the dark
water of grief; once the frenzy was past, she had got
over Jan's death. But why had she too been caught up in
the frenzy? Was it a longing for common ground that
found fulfillment in her dealings with Ulla? But if that
was the case why didn't she also share Ulla's conviction
that it had been suicide, or an abduction-and-murder
plot? Was it a desire for adventure? Was it megalomania?
There had been moments back then when she really

thought she was on the trail of something big. Whatever it was that had drawn her into that frenzy—where was it? Was there something within her that she had since suppressed? Something that had really yearned to be experienced, and perhaps still wished to be?

When Ilse finally heard the repeated ringing of the bell, it was seven o'clock and high time. There was no mirror in the room; Ilse opened the window and sought her image in the window. She resisted the temptation to adjust her hair or her face; her reflection was too vague and in any case she wasn't good with comb, mascara and lipstick. But she didn't avert her eyes from herself. She felt sorry for the woman that was her, always too inhibited to be entirely present wherever she happened to be. Except at home—she was homesick, even though she was a little ashamed of the meagerness of her domestic happiness with cats and books. She smiled ruefully at herself. The evening air was cool, she breathed deeply in and out. She summoned all her strength and went downstairs to join the others.

Six

Christiane had made a seating plan, and in front of each plate stood a little card with a name and a picture— a picture from the old days. The pictures were handed around and marveled at. "Look!"—"The beard!"— "The hair!"—"Did I look like that back then?"—"But you've changed too!"—"Where did you get the pictures?"

Ilse had not yet greeted anyone apart from Margarete and Henner, and did so now. Jörg seemed just as awkward as she felt herself. When he didn't return her hug, she thought at first that it was her fault. Then she told herself that in prison he had missed developments in etiquette and hadn't learned to hug by way of greeting.

His place was on one of the long sides of the table between Christiane and Margarete. Opposite him sat Karin, flanked by Andreas and Ulrich. Next to Andreas and Margarete, Ulrich's wife and Karin's husband sat facing each other; next to Ulrich and Christiane were Ilse and Henner. On one of the short sides Ulrich's daughter sat between Ilse and Henner, on the other a place was set for Marko Hahn, who could only come later. Karin tapped the glass with her fork and said, "Let us pray," waited until they had all got over their amazement and were quiet, and prayed. "Lord, stay with us, for evening is on its way and the day has declined."

Henner looked around; apart from Jörg and Andreas they had all lowered their heads—some had also closed their eyes. Jörg's lips moved as if he were joining in or saying his own secular, revolutionary grace.

" 'For evening is on its way'—does that mean that the Christians needed God more by night than by day? I'm not like that—I need help by day more than by night," Andreas said with mocking interest as soon as Karin was finished. His mockery suited him, it suited his gauntness, the angularity of his movements, his bald head and cold gaze. "And why 'and the day has declined'? Isn't evening being on its way and the day having declined one and the same thing?"

"That's what lawyers are like—they twist and turn your words in their mouths." Ulrich laughed. "But quite honestly, Karin, doesn't it ever get too much for you? Singing, praying, preaching, saying pious, clever things about everyone and everything? I know it's your job—my job sometimes gets too much for me as well."

"Your first meal in freedom—what do you think?" Christiane gave Jörg a friendly nudge with her elbow.

"Your first meal in freedom—a meal with grace." Andreas wouldn't let go. "What do you think about that?"

"It isn't my first meal in freedom. We ate this morning on the autobahn and in Berlin at lunchtime."

"That's why we didn't get here till this evening," Christiane explained. "I thought Jörg should get a bit of city air. His release came as such a surprise that they couldn't run the usual program. They took him out a bit the day before yesterday—that was it. No proper day release, no open prison. But do start—what are you waiting for?" She pushed the bowl of potato salad toward Karin, and the bowl of sausages toward Andreas.

"Thanks." Karin took the bowl. "I don't want to leave you without an answer. The hustle often gets too much for me, and not only because I'm actually rather slow. When I'm rushed, singing, praying and preaching don't really come from the heart any longer, they become a job that I have to do. That doesn't do God justice, and it does me no good."

"I call that a good answer." Ulrich nodded and put some potato salad on his plate. Pushing the bowl toward Ilse, he turned to Jörg. "I don't even need to ask you."

Annoyed, Jörg looked at Ulrich, then Christiane, then again at Ulrich. "What . . ."

"Whether it was ever too much for you. What was actually the worst thing about jail? That you weren't rushed, that you had too much time and not enough to do? That you were always in the same place? The other inmates? The food? No alcohol? No women? You were in solitary, I read somewhere, and you didn't have to work—that's half the battle, isn't it?"

Jörg struggled for an answer while already talking with his hands. Christiane intervened. "I don't think those are questions that should be asked right now. Let him settle in before you give him the third degree."

"Christiane, the eternal big sister. You know the first thing I remembered when your invitation arrived? How I met you both more than thirty years ago, you always by his side, always with one eye on what he happened to be doing. At first I thought you were a couple, before I worked out that you were the big sister looking after her little brother. Let's leave him aside for now. Karin has told us what things are like for her as a bishop. I'd be happy to tell you how my life with the labs is going, if you'd like to hear it, and he can tell us about his life in jail."

Ilse and Henner looked at each other. Ulrich's tone lightened. But in his words, as in Christiane's, there was a certain sharpness, as if they were both fighting a restrained battle. What were they fighting for?

"You don't want to hear anything about solitary confinement—none of you want to hear anything about that. And sleep deprivation and force-feeding and the insults and the isolation unit. Afterward, when I had won the battle for normal conditions of imprisonment"—Jörg laughed—"so, when prison conditions were normal . . . the noise was bad. Perhaps you think it's quiet in prison, but it's noisy. For every activity iron doors have to be opened and closed and iron passageways and iron steps have to be walked down. By day people shout at one another and at night they shout in their sleep. And then there's the radio and the peephole, and one person clattering on a typewriter, and someone else banging his dumbbells against the door." Jörg spoke slowly, haltingly, and with the random, agitated gestures that had startled Christiane in the morning and startled her again now. "You want to know what the worst thing is? That life is elsewhere. That you're cut off from it and rotting, and the longer you wait for afterward, the less afterward is worth."

"Did you ever imagine having to go to prison? I

mean, the way an employee imagines being fired or a doctor imagines contracting an illness? A professional risk? Or did you think you'd keep going and end up retiring as a terrorist, in the old terrorists' home, where young terrorists would look after you? Did you . . ."

"Has everyone got something in his glass?" Eberhard had a powerful voice, with which he effortlessly drowned out Ulrich. "I'm the oldest one here at the table, and I'm the one you should ask about retirement and old people's homes. Jörg is still young, and I raise my glass to the many active and fulfilled years of freedom that he still has ahead of him. To Jörg!"

"To Jörg!"

When they had all set their glasses back down, it was a moment before they started talking again. Karin's husband smilingly remarked to Ulrich's wife about her stubborn husband. Andreas ironically apologized to Karin; he had actually understood the prayer, he didn't know what had come over him. Christiane whispered to Jörg: "Talk to Margarete!" and Ilse and Henner asked Ulrich's daughter about school and what sort of work she planned to do afterward.

Ulrich wouldn't let go. "You're acting as if Jörg has leprosy and you're not allowed to talk about it. Why shouldn't I ask him about his life? He chose it—just as you chose yours and I chose mine. I actually think you're being arrogant."

Jörg started speaking again, still slowly, still haltingly. "So . . . I didn't think about old age. I didn't think beyond the end of each action or perhaps to the start of the next one. A journalist once asked me if a life outside the law was bad, and he couldn't understand that it wasn't bad. I think any life that you live now, in which you're not somewhere else in your thoughts, is good."

Ulrich looked around triumphantly. He nearly said, "Come on!" For a while he let the individual conversations continue. Ilse, who thought she remembered where the pictures on the place markers came from, asked Christiane. Yes, she had cut them from a collection made at Jan's funeral. Ilse asked Jörg if he remembered Jan, and was confused by the answer, "He's the best." Ulrich's daughter quietly asked Henner if he thought Jörg had turned homosexual in prison, and Henner answered just as quietly that he had no idea, but knew that in boarding schools, camps and prisons there was a kind of pragmatic homosexuality that disappeared again afterward. Christiane whispered to Jörg, who was eating in silence: "Ask Margarete how she found the house!"

But Ulrich preempted her. "I'm sure you remember your first case and your first sermon." He nodded to Andreas and Karin. "And Ilse her first lesson and Henner his first article. I will never forget my first bridge; I never put so much time and love into any later work, and learned something from it that has served me for life. What about your first murder, Jörg? Did it give you . . ."

"Stop it, Ulrich, please stop it!" his wife exploded.

Ulrich raised his arms in resignation and let them fall again. "OK, OK. If you think . . ."

Henner realized that he didn't know what to think, and when he looked around at the others he read in their faces that they didn't know either. He admired Ulrich for being so direct, so straightforward. Jörg's life was Jörg's life, just as their lives were their lives—perhaps Ulrich was right. At any rate, Ulrich could have an interested and engaged conversation with Jörg. He, Henner, could manage nothing but small talk.

After dessert Jörg got to his feet. "It's been years— what am I saying—it's been more than two decades since I had such a long, full day. Please forgive me for going to bed. We'll see one another again at breakfast tomorrow—many thanks to you all for coming, and sleep well." He walked around the table and shook hands with each of them. To the astonished Henner he said, "I think it was brave of you to come."

As he left the room, Christiane was about to stand up and go with him. Beneath Ulrich's scornful gaze she thought better of it.

Seven

Andreas had got to his feet when Jörg had said good-bye to him, and paused. "I think I should be . . ."

"Please, I don't want everyone leaving!" Christiane jumped to her feet and waved her hands around as if to press Andreas back down into his chair and keep the others in theirs. "It's ten o'clock, far too early for bed. Andreas, I'm so glad that you've finally met our old friends and they've met you—I'm sure you've had a hard day, but do stay awhile."

As if she were an officer whose soldiers wanted to desert, Henner thought. Why the fear that we would slip away?

Ingeborg was still bickering with her husband. "You can't talk to Jörg like that! Can't you see that he's exhausted? He's just got out of jail after twenty-something years, and instead of letting him pull himself together, you're wearing him out." She looked around as if expecting agreement.

Karin tried to be conciliatory. "Wearing him out—I didn't think that was what Ulrich was trying to do. But I also think that at the moment we should leave Jörg in peace with the past and give him courage for the future. Christiane, what are his plans?"

Ulrich didn't let Christiane answer. "In peace? If he's had an excess of anything over the past few years, it's peace. He's in his mid- or late fifties, as we all are, and his life was . . . What would you call it? Robbing banks and killing people, terrorism, revolution and prison— that was the life he chose for himself. And I'm not supposed to ask him what it was like? That's what old friends' reunions are for—you talk about the old days and tell one another what you've been doing since then."

"You know just as well as I do that it isn't a normal old friends' reunion. We're here to help Jörg find his way in life. And show him that life and people are glad to have him back."

"Karin, that's part of your job. But I'm not on a therapeutic mission. I'm happy to give Jörg a job. I also want to help him find one somewhere else. I would do that for any old friend, so it's the same for Jörg. The fact that he killed four people . . . If it isn't a reason to terminate the friendship, neither is it a reason to coddle him like a sensitive little soul."

"Therapeutic mission? I think my memory's a bit better than yours. No violence against individuals, and if there was, it wasn't hard missiles, just soft ones, tomatoes and eggs, but in the people's liberation struggle against imperialism and colonialism of course there were guns and bombs as well, and we, in the metropolitan centers of imperialism and capitalism, owe our solidarity to the liberation struggle, and solidarity means taking part in that combat—have you forgotten that we all used to talk like that? Not just Jörg, these people too." Karin pointed at the gathering. "And you too. Yes, with you it stayed words—you don't need to explain the difference between talking and shooting. But would it have stayed words if you'd grown up without a mother? If you had the same problems dealing with people as Jörg does? If you didn't have the gift of seizing life so resolutely and effectively?"

"The terrorists as our confused brothers and sisters?" Ulrich shook his head and made a face not only of rejection, but of revulsion. "Do you believe that too?" He looked around the group.

Ilse broke the silence. "I didn't talk of struggles in those days. I didn't talk at all. I brewed coffee with the girls and made stencils and printed up pamphlets. You didn't, Karin, and neither did you, Christiane—I admired and envied you for it. Jörg and the others who fought were the ones I admired. Yes, the struggle was nonsense. But everything was nonsense in those days. The Cold War and the secret services and the arms race and the real wars in Asia and Africa—when I think back to that, it strikes me as insane." She laughed. "Not that it's any better these days. The attacks and uprisings and wars since then—I can only think that the people who do that must be crazy. Jörg has put it behind him. Isn't that what matters?"

"Karin, I know you mean well. But it isn't true that Jörg wasn't loved when he was . . ."

Christiane stopped talking and listened. Footsteps came across the gravel, someone opened the front door, walked down the hall and opened the door to the drawing room. "I saw the light under the door and thought . . . I'm Marko."

Christiane got to her feet and greeted him, introduced him to the friends and the friends to him and dis-appeared into the kitchen to cook up some sausages for him. She did everything quickly, in a detached and busi-nesslike way. The friends, who knew the name Marko Hahn after they had been introduced but didn't know who he was or what connected him and Jörg, were slightly irritated; at the same time they were glad of the interruption. They stood up, opened the door and win-dows to the garden, cleared up, emptied the ashtrays, fetched new water and wineglasses, replaced the can-dles. "There's a gale a-brewin'," said Karin's husband, and Margarete stepped into the doorway and, after glancing at the sky and the wind-tossed treetops, pre-dicted a storm. Ilse came and stood next to her and put her arm around her, she herself didn't know why. Mar-garete laughed a warm laugh, put her arm around Ilse and drew her to her.

Suddenly it occurred to Andreas who Marko was. "You've done enough harm. If word reaches the press about our days here, you'll get a writ from me, one from which you will never recover." He had talked himself into action, left Marko, who was about to answer, standing where he was and turned to the startled Hen-ner. "I know you can do something. But as far as these days here are concerned, the same goes for you: not a word in the press. If you write anything about Jörg's first days in freedom and what he does and says, I'll tear you apart in public."

"You're right," said Eberhard to Margarete. "The weather's turning."

Marko grabbed Andreas by the arm. "We won't let

you and his sister lock him up. He didn't get out of prison for that. He didn't tough it out for that. The struggle goes on, and Jörg will take the place that suits him. We've waited for him long enough."

"Don't touch me!" When Andreas said it again, he was shouting. "Don't touch me!"

"Will you help me bring in the garden furniture before it starts raining?" Again Karin tried to make peace. But although the two men went outside together, folded the table and chairs and carried them into the house, they still stuck to their guns. Andreas talked about the pardon and its conditions and the threat of probation, Marko of the struggle that had to be fought and won, the struggle that was Jörg's life. Finally Karin sent Andreas in one direction and Marko in the other to look in the garden for lounge chairs.

Then the first drops fell. Karin peered around, looking for the two squabblers, then said to herself that they would find their way to the house without her and went inside. She would have liked to go to bed with her husband, would have liked to lay her head in the crook of his arm and her arm over his chest, open the window and listen to the rustle of the rain. But she couldn't run away from her mission to pacify and reconcile and heal. Ulrich was right in what he said about my mission, she thought, and she thought of Christiane, who had taken on an even greater one when only a child. She had been nine years old when her mother had died, and she had tried to take the place of her mother for her brother, three years younger than she, loving and punishing, comforting and distracting, cheering and urging. Karin was annoyed with herself for making the remark about Jörg being brought up without a mother; she had hurt Christiane. She would apologize to her, and perhaps by doing so entice her out of her nervous tension and into a conversation.

Then she heard, they all heard, the scream.

Eight

Ulrich and his wife knew immediately that their daughter had screamed. They looked around searchingly—where had the scream come from? Seeing the puzzled parents, the others also realized that they hadn't seen the daughter for quite some time. "When did she leave?"—"Where did the scream come from?"—"From the park?"—"From the house?"

Then they all heard the clamor in the hall. Ulrich tore open the door, his wife and the others following him. Standing in the upstairs hallway were the daughter, naked, and Jörg in his white nightshirt.

"You wuss. Fucking is fighting—wasn't that your motto? Fighting is fucking? Why are you always looking at my breasts when you can't get it up? You're not a man. You're a joke. You're probably a joke as a terrorist too, and they locked you up to stop you looking at women's breasts all the time. You're a voyeur. You're a joke and a voyeur." She put as much rejection, contempt and disgust into her voice as she could. But she sounded more despairing than disgusted, and then she burst into tears.

"I didn't look at your breasts. I want nothing of you. Leave me alone, please, leave me alone."

What a picture, Henner thought. The hall was only faintly lit by candles, shadows twitched on the walls, Dorle and Jörg's faces were indistinct, her nakedness and his nightshirt all the more present. Neither said anything; they were still facing each other, but antagonistically. It was a mysterious, ludicrous, wordless scene on a stage, with everyone craning his neck to see.

Christiane snapped at Ulrich. "Get your daughter off his back!"

"Don't make such a big deal of it!" But he went up the stairs, taking his jacket off, laid it around his daughter's shoulders and led her to the door at one end of the hallway.

Jörg looked around as if waking from a dream, staring after the man in his shirtsleeves and the naked young woman with the man's jacket thrown around her, as if he didn't know who they were, looked down into the hall and into the embarrassed faces of the guests, said nothing, slowly shook his head and walked, with the dragging gait that Christiane had already noticed that morning, to the door at the other end of the hallway. The stage was empty.

Christiane and Ingeborg looked as if they were about to run up and take care of their brother and daughter. Karin, feeling that this would make everything even more awful, put her arms around both of them and led them back to the table. "It's all a bit much this evening. For everyone and all the more for Jörg and our youngest. Things won't look so bad tomorrow."

"We're leaving tonight."

"Let her sleep it off. She may not even want to leave. She may not want to leave things like that, but somehow impose a kind of order on it all. She's a strong girl."

Marko saw her as a bit of a babe more than anything, and jabbed Andreas in the side with his elbow. "What's up with Jörg? Why chuck her out of bed? Does he want to be a Muslim and martyr—on earth, battle and prayer and women only in heaven, an endless supply of virgins?" He shook his head. "He's never . . ."

Andreas turned away without a word. But when he was about to climb the stairs, Jörg came toward him. He had taken off his nightshirt and put his jeans and shirt back on. "That was an unlovely situation, and I wouldn't like the evening to end with it." It was a great effort for him to look at Andreas; his eyes kept drifting away, and he kept forcing them back to look into Andreas's eyes. Then he walked over to Henner and Karin's husband, who were in conversation, and repeated the sentence. Andreas had followed him, Marko had joined them too and heard the sentence, and now they stood facing him waiting for him to continue. When they realized that he had prepared only one sentence, he realized that it wasn't enough. "I'm . . . I've cut a poor figure, I know. Christiane had a nightshirt made for my first night in freedom, because I like night-shirts and you can't get them anymore, and I put it on. I had no idea you would all see me in it." He realized that even that wasn't enough. "She and I . . . we had a mis-understanding, just a misunderstanding." Now it was OK. He had regretted what had happened, he had acknowledged that he had not cut a good figure, he had admitted that they had misunderstood each other—he had done his part, and the others should leave him alone. He looked at them all. "I'll have another glass of red wine."

Nine

Ulrich sat by his daughter's bed. She had pulled the covers up to her chin and turned her head away. Ulrich didn't see her crying, only heard it. He laid his hand on the covers, felt her shoulder and tried to give his hand a comforting, calming heaviness. When the tears subsided, he waited for a while and then said: "You mustn't feel humiliated. He's just the wrong one."

She turned her tear-stained face to him. "He hit me, not hard, but he did hit me. That's why I screamed."

"You were too much for him. He didn't want to hurt you—he only wanted to get rid of you."

"But why? I'd have done him good."

He nodded. Yes, his daughter had thought she would do Jörg good. Not that that had been her intention; she hadn't thrown herself at him to do him good. Or because she had suddenly fallen in love with him. She had wanted to sleep with the famous terrorist so that she could say she had slept with the famous terrorist. But she wouldn't have wanted to do it if she hadn't told herself she would do him good after all those years in jail.

He remembered how he had collected famous men. He had started with Rudi Dutschke. He was still a schoolboy—he skipped school, went to Berlin and didn't let up until he had met Dutschke and exchanged a few words with him about the struggle in the schools. The others thought he was very left-wing, and he put up with that and sometimes fell for it himself. But in fact he knew that all he wanted was to have experienced them in person: Dutschke, Marcuse, Habermas, Mitscherlich and finally Sartre. He was particularly proud of that one; again he simply set off, not by train this time but by car, and waited for two days outside Sartre's apartment building until on the third day he was able to talk to him and spend a few minutes with him in the café drinking espresso. Then a woman came to the table and he left—he was still annoyed about the fact that he hadn't recognized Simone de Beauvoir, and hadn't, with a charming remark, suggested to the pair that he join them for dinner. His French had been good back then.

How much is in the genes, he wondered. He had never told his daughter about his passion for collecting, so she couldn't have copied her passion for collecting from him, only inherited it. He remembered, a few years ago, seeing her threading new laces into her sneakers, always crosswise, on the left-hand shoe the lace leading to the right over the one leading to the left and on the right-hand shoe the lace leading to the left over the one leading to the right, so that in the end they were laced in a mirror image of each other. He himself did exactly the same thing and he had never done it in front of her or even in her presence.

"Will you please open the window, Papa?"

He got to his feet, opened both casements of the window, let the cool, damp air and the rustle of the rain into the room and sat back down by the bed.

His daughter looked at him as if trying to read in his face the answer to the question that she had not yet even asked. Then she summoned her strength. "Can we leave tomorrow morning? Before I have to see any of the others?"

"Let's see how we feel tomorrow morning."

"But if I don't want to see the others, I don't have to—promise?"

When was the last time he had turned down a request from her? He couldn't remember. But neither could he remember a request aimed at escape. She had always wanted to have something, a dress, a piece of jewelry, a horse, a trip, and he had taken her requests as an expression of her hunger for life: she couldn't get enough of life and all that it offered. Hunger for life, vital energy—didn't the two belong together? Had his daughter not always looked for challenges? He had been happy to give her the horse because at seven she was a bold equestrian, and the trip with her friend to America, because at the age of sixteen they both wanted to explore the country by Greyhound bus.

"I've always admired you for your courage." He laughed. "You're a spoiled brat, I know, but you're not a coward."

She couldn't hear him anymore. She had gone to sleep. No pouting now; her face had a sweet, peaceful, childlike expression. My angel, Ulrich thought. My angel with the blond curls and the full lips and the high breasts. Ulrich had never understood fathers who were sexually attracted to their daughters before puberty, or Humbert Humbert, who loves not the woman in Lolita but the child. But he felt for the fathers and teachers who were overwhelmed by the femininity of their daughters or pupils. No, he didn't just feel for them; he was one of them. Again and again it took all his strength actually to look at his daughter when she talked to him and not to look at her lips, not to stare at her bouncing bosom when she came downstairs, or her bottom when she went upstairs in front of him. And in the summer, when her blouses and shirts revealed the tops of her breasts and her walk not only made her breasts dance but made her skin quiver in little waves—it was a torment, a sweet, proud torment, but a torment nonetheless.

Did Jörg have no eyes in his head? Or was he so stubborn that he could see beauty only in female revolutionaries, in whom everything was ideologically sound? Or had he turned gay in prison? Or kicked the habit? Simply kicked the habit? Ulrich was glad that nothing had happened between his daughter and Jörg. He didn't know much about her sexual experiences. He hoped she would experience love and happiness and not come to harm. But he couldn't imagine Jörg being the right one for her. But glad as he was, by rejecting his daughter, Jörg had insulted him. That was foolish, and it was even more foolish that he wanted to avenge himself. He knew it, but it didn't help. Besides, Jörg and Christiane had always been arrogant in their treatment of him, and he had always hated them for it. But he hadn't known what to do with his hatred.

He listened. His daughter was snoring quietly. The rain rustled in the leaves of the trees and on the gravel in front of the house. Sometimes it gurgled in the gutter. A saxophone played; it sounded as if the slow, sad tune came from a long way away. Ulrich wearily hoisted himself from the chair, closed one casement, left the other open a crack, tiptoed to the door and carefully opened and closed it. Now he heard the saxophone more clearly—it was coming from downstairs. He knew the tune, but couldn't remember what it was called and who played it. The old days—the more time he spent with his old friends, the more clearly he remembered what he and they had wanted and done back then, the more alien the past became to him.

That one's life could slip away like that. He tried to remember his childhood, his school, his first marriage. He assembled images, events, moods. He couldn't say, That's what it looked like in the old days, that happened in the old days, that's what I felt like in the old days. But outwardly he saw it as a film, and he felt cheated. Then he grew annoyed. Why must I too dig around in the past? I don't normally do that. I'm a practical person. I concern myself with now and with tomorrow.

He wouldn't leave the next day.

Ten

When the saxophone had faded away and Christiane had clicked the off button on her little portable player, most people took their leave. "Good night."—"Sleep well."—"See you tomorrow morning."

Ilse stayed sitting at the table, although she realized that Jörg and Marko would have preferred not to have her there. Marko wished he could be rid of Christiane as well, but she wouldn't have budged for anything in the world, and Jörg kept her at the table, turning toward her as he turned toward Marko, filling her glass as well. The tension among the three of them was so powerful that Ilse sensed an exciting electric crackle and simply refused to yield to her shyness, which was urging her to disappear unnoticed.

At first she listened. Then she found what was being said uninteresting. The words that Jörg, Christiane and Marko exchanged seemed to her as random as the pieces with which players do battle on a board. The struggle among the three of them was reflected not in words, but in their voices, expressions, gestures. In Christiane's shrill aggression, in Marko's brown-nosing. Marko presented himself as the inevitable winner, and Christiane grew more and more desperate. Jörg spoke no less than the other two, and no less loudly. Increasingly, Ilse understood that he wasn't really fighting. The other two were fighting. They were fighting for his soul.

And he was enjoying it. It wasn't just the wine that loosened his tongue, turned his face red and freed his gestures. It wasn't just the warm candlelight that softened his wrinkles. What brought him to life was being at the center of things and sensing how important, how precious he was to Christiane and Marko. It rejuvenated him. So much so that he kept spurring them both not to give up their fight over him.

"He's still little more than a child," Jörg said soothingly to Christiane, who accused Marko of nearly costing Jörg his pardon with his welcome address at the conference on violence, in response to which Marko had to present himself as the young but alert revolutionary who had every right to woo Jörg.

"You would like to incapacitate me," Jörg said reproachfully to Christiane, who didn't want him to meet the organizers of the conference, whereupon she had to assure him how reflective and superior she thought he was.

Marko wouldn't let go. "I don't want you to get involved with everything and everyone. But we need you. We don't know how to fight the system. We argue and argue, and sometimes a few of us organize an action, and there's a fire outside the state attorney's office or an alarm in the station, and the trains are late, but that's kids' stuff. If we joined forces with our Muslim comrades we could really get things going. They with their power and we with what we know about this country—together we could really strike where it hurts. But then along come people who say, Don't do it

with them, we might as well be working with the far
right; and a few say, exactly, why not work with them,
and then there are the old discussions you know so well,
whether it should be violence against people or against
property or no violence at all—we need someone with
authority. The other RAF people ate humble pie and
wept and repented and apologized—not you. You have
no idea what kind of authority you have."

Jörg shook his head. But only because he wanted to
hear more: about how steadfast he had been in jail and
about the admiration of the young members and his
authority over them and his responsibility. Yes, Marko
assured him, his authority meant responsibility, and he
couldn't leave the young ones in the lurch.

How could Christiane respond to that? By saying he
should take his time. "You haven't been out of jail for
twenty-four hours and . . ."

"Take his time," sneered Marko. "Take his time?
He's had to take his time for twenty-three years. He has
held out for twenty-three years to become the model
that he is now. You'd have sent Nelson Mandela from
Robben Island to the Bavarian mountains for a spring
holiday—am I right?"

Nelson Mandela? Ilse looked at Jörg—he gave a
slightly embarrassed smile, but didn't protest. Was his
hunger for recognition so great? How starved would I
be after twenty-three years? Could I resist Marko? He
was good. When he looked straight at Jörg with his
open face, his blue eyes, it was as if he were trustingly
placing his youth at Jörg's feet. She wondered whether
or not Jörg believed in a revival of the struggle against

the system, a collaboration with Al Qaeda and himself as a role model—he believed in Marko's admiration, and believed that Marko was not alone in it.

"Don't you remember how often you used to talk about your longing for nature? For forests and meadows, the young greenery in spring and the colors in autumn, the smell of freshly mown grass and rotting leaves? And your longing for the sea—sometimes you said that after your release you would walk along the beach and look at the waves until you had the evenness of the waves inside you. And sometimes you dreamed of a big orchard, under which you would lie on a lawn chair in the spring, wrapped in a blanket, protected against the cold—don't let them take that dream away!"

With Marko at the table, Jörg's longing and dreams were embarrassing to him. "I was desperate at the time, Christiane. I see more clearly now that I have a twofold responsibility, not just to me, but to those who believe in me. But the storm has passed, and I would like to walk another little way with you, through the forest and across the meadow." He smiled. "Shall we?"

And again Christiane was immediately reconciled. She had been oversensitive. Jörg had not revealed to Marko his longing for nature, which he had shared with her. She got to her feet before Jörg did so, and when he too was standing, she took his arm and clung to him like a lover.

"Do we need a flashlight?"

"No, I know all the paths."

"I'm sure you'll all be in bed when we get back. Empty the bottle, and sleep well." Jörg waved with his left hand and put his right around Christiane's waist. They opened both wings of the door to the garden, stepped onto the terrace and were swallowed by the night.

"Well, then." Marko filled Ilse's glass and his own from what was left in the bottle. "Want one?" He offered her a cigarette.

"No thanks."

Marko took his time lighting his cigarette. "You looked at me all evening as if you were wondering whether I really believed what I said. Or whether I was in my right mind. Believe me, I'm in my right mind, and I believe what I say. On the other hand I wonder whether you and your kind understand what's happening to the world. You probably think September Eleventh was just some crazy Muslim affair. No, without September Eleventh none of the good things that have happened over the past few years would have happened. The new attentiveness to the Palestinians, still the key to peace in the Middle East, and to the Muslims, still a quarter of the world's population, the new sensitivity to the threats in the world, from the economic to the ecological, the realization that exploitation has a price that is always rising— sometimes the world needs a shock to come to its senses. Like people—after having his first heart attack, my father is at last living as sensibly as he should always have lived. With some people it takes two or three."

"Some die of heart attacks."

Marko stubbed out his half-smoked cigarette, drained his glass and got to his feet. "Ah, Ilse—that's your name, Ilse?—if anyone dies of a heart attack today, it's their own fault. Sleep well."

Eleven

In her room Ilse sat in the dark for a while before lighting the candle and opening her notebook.

"He's the best"—she couldn't get Jörg's remark about Jan out of her head. Did he mean a different Jan? If he meant their mutual friend, "he's the best" sat ill with Jörg's words at the funeral, and would have been peculiar enough. "He's the best" didn't fit at all. Unless their mutual friend Jan really hadn't killed himself back then, but escaped his old life to start a new one, a life as a terrorist, which he was still living today. Then Jörg's contempt at the funeral had been only playacting and his admiration today was genuine. And then Jan had earned the admiration: a terrorist who hadn't allowed himself to be caught.

Ilse remembered all her research in those days and imagined how Jan had deceived them all. He must have bribed or blackmailed the undertakers. The undertakers had picked him up in France, brought him to Germany, put him in a coffin and buried him. He was also able to get hold of the other corpse, which the French pathologist had found on the table, the one on which he had performed the autopsy. That the corpse had been presented to him in sweatshirt and jeans rather than a suit was a glitch—perhaps Jan had forgotten to bring a second suit. Someone else must have helped Jan: a doctor, or a nurse.

The French police had received an anonymous phone call back then. It was six o'clock, after a cold night, the fresh morning of a sunny spring day. A policeman rode his motorbike to the rocky coast and found the car parked in the given place. A 2CV—out of a mixture of nostalgia and snobbery Jan refused himself a Mercedes like the ones driven by his friends at his firm. The engine had used up all the gas and hadn't been running for a while, the windows were clear, and the policeman could clearly see Jan, leaning back and against the window, eyes and mouth open, hands in his lap. The policeman could also see what had happened; a tube led from the exhaust pipe to the passenger side and through the carefully sealed window into the car. He opened the door, and Jan slipped from the seat, out of the car and onto the ground. He looked as dead as only a dead person could look, and felt like one too: cold skin, greenish color, no breath. The policeman informed headquarters and called an ambulance and took photographs until it arrived: the car, the tube on the exhaust pipe, the tube at the window, the rock on the accelerator, Jan on the ground beside the car, Jan's face from above and from the front and from the side.

Ilse and Ulla had looked at them again and again. And they had, when they were in Normandy, heard the story from the policeman. His name was Jacques Beaume, he had three children, he was very sympathetic and willing to tell the story in all its details and patiently answer questions. Wasn't it suspicious that the caller had remained anonymous? No, it was Sunday, and the caller didn't want to waste his time as a witness. Why had a second ambulance come after the first? The emergency services are all switched to the police frequency, and sometimes one snatched another's mission away. Jacques Beaume sat with Ilse and Ulla, first at the police station and then in the café, until they could imagine everything.

Jan leans against the car and waits until the tank is empty. The night is dark. The clouds shroud moon and stars and reflect no light—there is no town for miles around. In the distance Jan makes out the light of a lighthouse, no brighter than a bright star, with a little beam of light regularly flashing and vanishing.

A vicar's son, interested in theology as a schoolboy and philosophy as a student, dedicated throughout his life to doing what is right—Jan's thoughts pass from the starry sky that he can't see, to the moral law that he can't feel, to the step that he will take: leaving wife and children. And as in the past weeks when he thought about it, he again consoles himself with the thought that they will never learn about what he is doing. That he will be dead to them. That anyone who is dead can only be mourned. That anyone who kills himself cannot be reproached, only pitied. That he gives those left behind not the pain of abandonment but the pain of having someone torn from them, a pain caused not by people but by death, not a pain that we resist but one that we have learned to accept. And he goes on thinking about his new life and the power he will have in it, the power of the phantom whose identity no one knows and whose trail leads nowhere. His deeds can be all the bolder. He will become part of the story, first as someone anonymous, and later perhaps with his true identity when he reveals who has forced the system to its knees and wrested justice from it. From the murky business whose mandate his firm imposed upon him, and whose documents he destroyed, he has already leeched a million.

Jan shivers, even though the softly ticking, gently vibrating car gives off warmth. He knows that he will soon feel much colder.

The engine coughs and dies. But the night isn't quiet. The sea's waves come rushing in, break crashing against the cliffs and, where they take sand and gravel with them, run hissing back to the sea. Sometimes a gull cries. Jan looks at his watch. It's three o'clock; the others will be here any minute. Or what if only one comes?

Then Jan hears the car. He hears it getting louder as it drives over the brow of a hill, then he sometimes sees the headlights, switched to parking, and then it's quieter, when it goes into a dip. Where the path leads off the country road and toward the cliffs, it stops. Jan hears a car door slam. So only one of them has come.

The French comrades have sent a woman. She's friendly, matter-of-fact, succinct. "You know if you're unlucky you'll die?"

"Yes." Jan won't die. He knows it.

"You have to show me the vein in your arm."

Jan takes off his jacket and lays it on the car roof, then unbuttons his shirtsleeve and pushes it up. With an encouraging gesture she gives him a flashlight. He grits his teeth and catches her in the beam. She takes out a syringe. "Valium first." He looks away as she pricks his vein. Even before she's finished, he looks. She doesn't take very long; the syringe is unusually large. Then the woman is finished and presses cotton wool to the prick. "Now the Cardiogreen." No one had mentioned that. But the second injection happens quickly.

Jan buttons up his sleeve, puts on his jacket and sits down in the car. She runs the beam of the flashlight across the ground and makes sure that no cotton wool, none of the packaging of the syringe or the ampoule has fallen. She stands in the open door and tells him what he is to do next. "In fifteen minutes you'll be asleep. At six you will be so cold, your breathing so shallow, that the police, if they aren't very accurate, will think you're dead. In fact you'll hardly be breathing. Why should the police be very precise? They'll call the ambulance." She laughs. "The Cardiogreen was my idea. It makes really lovely corpses." She lifts his increasingly heavy eyelids, shines the flashlight into his eyes and strokes his cheek. "At half past six, quarter to seven, our ambulance will collect you. Bonne chance!" She closes the door and goes.

Suddenly he is frightened. Suddenly something that is only supposed to look like death feels like real death. His life is ending, and what comes after is no *longer his life, but someone else's. If it comes—Jan no longer knows that he isn't going to die. You can't play with death. It won't be joked with. It . . .*

Full of the terror of death, Jan loses consciousness.

Ilse snapped her notebook shut. She would have liked to drink one more glass of red wine, but she was afraid of the silent, dark house and didn't dare go to the kitchen. When she was lying in bed she was afraid of going to sleep, as if by sleeping she were cavorting on the face of death. Or do we actually do that every time we go to sleep? And what about taking one's leave? When we die for others and at the same time want to go on living?

Then she too had fallen asleep.

Twelve

Ilse should not have been afraid of the silent, dark house. In the kitchen, Christiane sat at the table by the light of a candle, drank one last glass of red wine and one more and wondered how to hold the new day together better than the old one. Nothing had worked as she had planned. Of course Jörg should find the recognition that he had lacked for so long. But not from Marko—Christiane had always kept well away from the supporter scene, and thwarted their contact with Jörg wherever possible. Jörg was to find recognition among his old friends first of all, then through lectures, interviews, talk-show appearances and finally with an autobiography with a renowned publishing house. He had what it took, she knew he did, and she also knew that the public likes people who have been through hell and have thought about it and learned from it. If he relied on Marko, he would forfeit the chance of a lifetime. And why wasn't he interested in Margarete, who, with her warmth and cheerfulness, was exactly what he needed? Since meeting Margarete nine years before, she knew that she was the right one for Jörg. Margarete had also heard a lot about Jörg over the course of the years and even shown an interest in visiting him in jail. However, Christiane had never taken her to see the imprisoned Jörg; she had wanted to save her up for the free one.

Now Jörg was free and it could finally get going. But nothing had got going. And the nightshirt—it was supposed to make Jörg happy, and instead it had made him ridiculous. He must hate her for it.

How defenseless we are on sleepless nights! Exposed to the stupid thoughts that our waking mind would immediately resolve, the hopelessness defeated by small successes with clothes washing, car parking or the consoling of friends, the sadness from which we wrest victories in the exhaustion of playing tennis, running, or lifting weights. On sleepless nights we turn on the television or reach for a book, just so that, even though we might not fall asleep, our eyes close over the pictures and pages, and we fall victim once again to stupid thoughts, to hopelessness and sadness. Christiane didn't even have a television or a book. She had red wine, which didn't help. How was she to get a better grip on the day to come? She had no idea.

But she had to do it. If she didn't help Jörg better through the new day, how could she hope to bring him into a new and better life? He who had never had a life, a real life with work and colleagues and a regular address, but was always setting off again, always wanting to be somewhere different, wanting to do something different from wherever he happened to be and whatever he happened to be doing. She had to teach him to live.

She shouldn't have encouraged him to keep leaving back then. It had made her proud how skillfully her little brother dreamed himself into other times and worlds and how vividly he talked of them. She had been moved by the nobility of the deeds he performed in his fantasy, with Falk von Stauf at the relief of Marienburg, with T. E. Lawrence at the liberation of the Arabs, with Rosa Parks in the fight against racial segregation. Didn't that show that he was a good boy? Then his fantasy turned to the present and the future and turned from "Oh, if only I had" into "Oh, if only I could" and "I should." And she had given him her approval in that as well. That he couldn't accept the badness of the world, that he wanted to fight for justice, confront the oppressors and exploiters and help the hurt and the humiliated—how could she not have given him her approval for that? But she shouldn't have done it. She certainly shouldn't have let him realize how she yearned to see him as the hero of great deeds.

She knew that mothers could destroy their sons with their expectations. But she wasn't Jörg's mother, she certainly wasn't one of those mothers who didn't have a life of their own, who expected nothing of themselves and had to expect everything of their son, and she loved Jörg anyway, whether he performed great deeds or not. No, she couldn't have harmed Jörg with her expectations. Or could she?

Or had she had too much of a life of her own? Should she have abandoned her medical studies, which she had begun when Jörg was going through puberty? Later, when he drifted out of his studies, she had been working as a specialist and had once again had only a little time for him. For a long time she didn't notice what was coming. By the time she did, it was too late.

She shook her head. Enough of the past. How can I

give Jörg a future? The best offer he had received was a traineeship in a publishing house. Well-paid traineeship—she didn't like that. Traineeships were hard to come by, and trainees worked for little money. The publisher only wanted to satisfy his romantic longing for revolution and terrorism, adorn himself with Jörg whatever the cost might be, but he wasn't really interested in Jörg's work. Did Henner know of anything for Jörg on a newspaper? Karin in the church? Ulrich in his labs? But Jörg wouldn't put on white overalls and cast crowns. He wouldn't have to either, if he played his cards right on his first talk-show appearance. He needed a coach. But would he listen to a coach?

She was anxious about the next few weeks. What would he do when she was at work? Not risk going out among people and into the street and stay at home? Or, avid for life and the world, commit one idiocy after another? She had employed their neighbors' son to familiarize Jörg with the computer and the Internet. In the guest room, Jörg's room, she had put the manuscripts and books from over thirty years before, when he was working on his master's degree. He hadn't wanted to go on working on it in jail. Maybe now that he was free? But she didn't believe that. In her anxiety she saw him in one of those shiny synthetic tracksuits, shambling through the streets that the unemployed roamed with dogs and cigarettes and beer cans, aimless, goalless, spiritless.

She knew she should be in bed. How could she do proper justice to the new day if she was tired and hung over? She got up and looked around. She stacked up the dirty crockery beside the sink; the sticky pots and pans stood on the stove. Christiane sighed, shocked by the extent of the task and relieved because, unlike the Jörg task, it was manageable. She lit more candles, put on water, filled the basin partway with cold water, squirted in dishwashing liquid, scraped the last bits of sausage and lettuce leaves off the plates and set one after the other into the sink. When the water was boiling, she poured it in and put more on to boil. Glasses, plates, bowls, cutlery, then pots and pans—it was no trouble, her head grew clearer and her heart calmer.

Then she felt she was being watched, and looked up. Henner was leaning in the doorway, T-shirt over his jeans and hands in his back pockets.

Thirteen

"How long have you been watching me?" She bent again over the pan, which refused to be cleaned.

"For two pans."

She nodded and went on rinsing. He stayed where he was and went on watching her. She wondered how she could endure his gaze. Did he recognize in her the woman he had liked back then? How did he recognize her, admiringly or pityingly, or with horror?

"The way you push your hair back behind your ear with your little finger sticking out when you're working —you used to do it exactly like that back then. And the way you turn from the hip where other people take a little step to the left or to the right. And the way you ask questions, blunt and serious and without any kind of flattery." So that I immediately start feeling guilty. No, thought Henner, you haven't changed. And the way I react to you hasn't changed either.

Henner saw the gray in Christiane's brown hair, the tear sacs under her eyes, the deep wrinkles above the base of her nose and from her nostrils to the corners of her mouth. He saw the liver spots on her hands and the fact that her freckles had lost their luster. He saw that Christiane did nothing for her figure, no sport, no gymnastics, no yoga. He saw it, and it didn't bother him. The fact that she was a few years older than him had excited him back then. The fact that it had excited him back then now made him a few years younger.

"What really happened back then?"

She didn't interrupt her work and didn't look up. "What are you talking about?"

Henner couldn't believe that it was supposed to be a serious question, and didn't reply. But after a while she asked once more, again without interrupting her work or looking up. "What do you want to know?"

He sighed, pulled away from the door, bent down to the boxes of mineral water, took a bottle and left. "Good night, Christiane."

She finished rinsing, cleaned the stove, wiped the table and let the water drain away. Then she dried, even though everything could have dried by itself. Then she sat down and poured herself another glass. All the rinsing and drying and preparing hadn't helped. She had to talk to Henner. He was too powerful as a journalist and too important for Jörg's future for her to allow herself to alienate him. She had to answer his questions. But what was she supposed to tell him? The truth?

She blew out the candles, walked through the hall, up the stairs and across the corridor to Henner's room. Light shone from under the door. She didn't knock. She opened the door quietly and walked in. Henner was in bed, his head and pillow resting against the wall, reading by candlelight. He looked up, calm and willing. Yes, she had liked his calm back then and his willingness to get involved with her, with her desires, thoughts, moods. There was something breezy about his willingness—it was open to everybody. Or did she just fear that? She found the willingness and calm in his face, in his attentive eyes, his big mouth with its narrow lips, his determined chin.

"You'll ruin your eyesight."

He lowered the book. "No, that's one of the false truths that we were taught as children, like oil on burns and charcoal for diarrhea."

"What are you reading?"

"A novel. About two journalists, male and female, their rivalry, their love, their separation." He laid the book on the chair beside the bed, on which the candle stood, and laughed. "The author and I were once together, and I want to know whether she wrote about me before someone mentions it."

"Did she?"

"Yes, but so far no one will notice apart from me."

Christiane hesitated before she asked. "Can I sit down on the foot of the bed? Then I can lean against the wall."

Henner nodded and curled up his legs. "Be my guest." Then he looked at her in attentive silence.

"I wasn't just saying that. I really don't know what you want to know."

He looked at her incredulously. "Christiane!"

But she looked seriously back. "So much happened back then."

He couldn't believe what she was saying. Was her experience of that summer so different from his? Wasn't it the summer of her love, as it was for him?

Since Henner and Jörg had been friends, Jörg had raved about her—there was no better word—his beautiful, brittle big sister. She was always kind to Henner, but he sensed that she didn't perceive him as a person, just as her little brother's friend, who did him good or harm. Until that summer. Until she suddenly took him seriously. He didn't know why it happened; he was supposed to bring her home in the car, a breakdown turned a fifteen-minute shared drive into half a night together and after that everything was different. They went together to see Marcuse and Dutschke, Deep Purple and José Feliciano, cuddled in the cinema and the swimming pool and made plans for two weeks in Barcelona, a brief summer of anarchy. Then they slept together, and in the middle of it she pulled away from him, stood up, grabbed her clothes and ran from the room. For weeks he tried to get hold of her and talk to her. She made herself unapproachable to him.

Yes, a lot had happened in that summer. But just one thing still left him asking questions more than thirty years later. Couldn't she see that herself? All right, then. "Why, when we were making love, did you suddenly leap to your feet and run away?"

Christiane closed her eyes. How she would have loved to present him with a lie. Even one that put her in a bad light. Even one that was embarrassing to her. But none occurred to her. So she had to tell the truth, although she knew he wouldn't understand it. He wouldn't understand anything. "It was at our place, you remember? In my room, my bed. I thought Jörg was away for the weekend, but he came home on Saturday and suddenly he was standing in the doorway—you weren't aware of it, but I saw him and saw his face when he understood and took a step back and closed the door again."

Henner waited for a while. "And?"

"And? I knew you wouldn't understand. Neither can I help you with the fact that Jörg and I . . . For a while he liked to provoke me with that stupid saying of his, 'And now, sis, what about a little bit of incest,' but nothing came of it. Still, I betrayed him, when you and I . . ." Christiane opened her eyes and looked questioningly at Henner. "You don't understand anything, do you? What mattered to me was only him, like what matters to a mother is only her son. All right, the mother still has her husband but not the way she has her son. Her husband belongs to yesterday, her son belongs to today—the fact that he alone existed for me kept him in the world, and when I betrayed him with you, he fell from the world, and I ran, but I couldn't catch up with him. It was too late, I couldn't make amends for what I had done."

Henner looked at her, saw the sadness in her face; because he didn't understand her, saw the hope that he might still understand her. He saw the exhaustion of futility; she had made sacrifice after sacrifice for her brother and achieved nothing, prevented nothing, encouraged nothing. He saw, even now, the obstinacy with which she thought she could catch him, with which she ran and ran to be there at the right moment. "For his sake did you . . . You did have relationships with men, didn't you? Were you married? Are you divorced?"

She shook her head. "I always attracted my young

colleagues, in the hospital or at conferences, and eventually they realized that I couldn't be what they were looking for, and I didn't want to. Then I sometimes had to send them away, because they were too weak to go; you know, the young ones I attracted were often the soft, weak ones, and sometimes they simply drifted away. I've met a few of them years later with their young wives—a nurse will have snapped them up, or a medical technician, and they've been a little embarrassed and shown me pictures of their children." Christiane smiled apologetically at Henner. "You mustn't think it wasn't lovely with you back then, or that I didn't like you. But it wasn't the most important thing. It was never the most important thing. There was no one I liked more than you."

Apart from Jörg, Henner thought, and what she said to comfort him just made him sad. If only she really had loved someone else! But he said nothing and nodded.

She bent down to him, kissed him on the mouth and stood up. "Sleep well."

"Why did Jörg say it was brave of me to come?"

"He said that?"

"Yes."

She stood by the bed and looked at him thoughtfully. "I don't know. Perhaps he said it to everyone. Perhaps he just wanted to say something kind. Don't worry about it."

Fourteen

But she couldn't help worrying about it. She was sure Jörg hadn't said it to everyone and hadn't meant it kindly. There was a challenge in his words, a threat. As if the next day weren't going to be awkward enough!

In the corridor she leaned against the wall. She could have slept standing, she was so tired. The conversation with Henner had taken more out of her than she had expected. Not being understood can be such an effort! But she had had no choice—she had had to say what she had said. And now she had to talk to Jörg.

No light came from his room. But he wasn't asleep. When she opened the door a crack, he immediately asked with suspicion and defensiveness in his voice: "Hello?"

She slipped into the room. "It's me."

"What's going on?" The matches he reached for fell from the chair to the floor, and he went on looking for them on the floor, cursing.

"I don't need any light. I just want to know what you meant when you told Henner it was brave of him to come."

"I need light, though." He found the matches, lit the candle and sat down on the edge of the bed. "I think it was brave of him to first make me end up in jail and then celebrate my release."

"He made you end up in jail?"

"Yes, he made me end up in jail. Apart from Dagmar and Wolf he was the only one who knew about Mother's cabin in the Odenwald, and both of them, Dagmar and Wolf, were arrested long after I was. When I went to fetch guns and money the cops were waiting for me."

"You can't know who Dagmar and Wolf talked to."

He rolled his eyes and spoke with the controlled patience with which adults react to the nonsensical objections of children. "I know they didn't talk to anyone, OK?"

"What do you plan to do?"

"Nothing. I just want to ask Henner how he felt back then. Everyone wants to know how I've felt about this and that—now I want to know too."

"Ulrich asked you; no one else did. Henner barely spoke."

"Then he can speak when he answers my question." Jörg gave his sister a hostile look. "Don't keep humiliating me. You tried to humiliate me over Ulrich and Marko, and now you want to humiliate me again over Henner. I answer other people's stupid questions because I understand why they are curious, but in that case they should answer my stupid questions too. I'm not doing anything to Henner. I'm not accusing him of anything. It was war, he decided which side he was on and he acted accordingly. I like him better than those goody-goodies who understand everything and everyone and never get their hands dirty. Useful idiots, but idiots nonetheless. No, I don't want to have an argument with him; I just want to know from him how he felt."

"But there will be an argument."

He smiled smugly. "Not from me, Tia, not from me." He got up, lifted his nightshirt a few inches and bowed ironically. "Be not afraid, your Royal Highness, your servant will cause you no shame. Particularly now that he wears your mantle. You're a treasure." He took her in his arms.

She laid her head against his chest. "Don't screw things up with Henner. He has a lot of influence and goodwill, he can help you. Who cares what happened thirty years ago. You have to live for the future, not in the past." He had called her Tia, and she wanted to call him Kiddo as she used to, and as their mother had done. But she felt that he had turned away from her as she spoke.

He still kept his arms around her, but the intimacy had gone. Then he rubbed her back. "Don't humiliate me, Christiane. I don't need anybody, no Henner, no Karin, no Ulrich. I get by with little—that's something I learned in jail. OK, I dream of holidays that I can't afford on Social Security. Do you think you'll take me with you sometime?" He pushed her from him, so that he could look into her face.

She was crying.

Fifteen

When everyone was asleep, Margarete woke up. When Jörg had left the table early she too had said good-bye to the group, gone to the garden house, where she lived alone, and gone to bed. Now she had been awoken by the pains in her left hip. Memories of an accident many years before. They woke her every night.

She turned onto her side, put her feet on the floor and sat up. Her hip hurt just as much sitting as lying. But the pain no longer spread into her left side and her left leg. She knew she should do exercises, stretch her hip, side and leg. Take the tablets she had forgotten before going to sleep.

Instead she looked out the window. The rain had stopped, the sky was clear, the moon shone on the park. It also shone on her feet. They gleamed quite white on the dark floorboards. She took it as a challenge to get up, go downstairs and walk outside the door. Every footstep was difficult. It wasn't just her hip. Since a doctor had treated her with cortisone she had grown fat. But losing weight would require more discipline than she had or wanted to have.

The house and the nearby village were in darkness. Only the moon and stars gleamed, the constellations overwhelmingly clear and bright, the Milky Way extravagantly generous, the moon contentedly sedate.

Margarete recalled holidays in the south, when, having grown up under a city-bright night sky, she first saw the starry sky in all its glory. Distance has nothing to do with it, she thought. It's all here.

On slow, cautious footsteps she set off. She wasn't afraid of nails or broken glass; she herself had removed rubbish and rubble around the house, and kept the paths clear. But walking on bare feet was unfamiliar and made her insecure—what would her feet feel next? Then it made her curious. Would the next thing be smooth earth, firm as stone, but slightly springy? Or gravel, resistant, prickly, tickling? Or a dry branch, breaking with a crack? Margarete's favorite path through the park was overgrown with grass, and she was already looking forward to the soft stalks beneath her feet.

She walked past the house. When she and Christiane had discovered the property two years before, she had immediately wanted the garden house for herself. Not because it was dry and the house was damp and moldy—she hadn't known that at the time. The house had too much history for Margarete, too much stale and wasted life. The damp and the mold only later confirmed to her that it was drenched in too much human smell, and spoiled by it. Now Margarete thought she could also sense the vibration of the guests, as if it were oozing from the house. Their good intentions, their sense of duty, their simultaneous involvement and withdrawal, the lies they served up to themselves and one another, their embarrassment, their helplessness. Margarete didn't look down on any of the guests; over the years she had experienced the whole spectrum of reactions to any closeness between Jörg and Christiane, and Christiane was her friend. Perhaps, she said to herself, I'm not being fair to the guests. Perhaps I'm seeing something in them that isn't even there. But we'll see tomorrow.

By the time Margarete and Christiane met, Jörg's trial was already a good few years in the past. At first Christiane didn't explain why she was away for a whole day every two weeks; she had to get hold of something, sort something out, see about something. Those were the months when both women thought they could be more than good friends to each other, and when Christiane got up and left at five in the morning, Margarete stayed in bed, fearful and sad. Later, when they both knew their love was a mistake and stayed in their shared apartment anyway, Christiane came out with the story of herself and Jörg. "I know he's my brother and not my lover, but back then I thought I could be open with you only when I'd come clean about him. But I couldn't do it. I didn't tell him you and I were together, and I didn't tell you that he existed. Silly, isn't it?" She smiled, embarrassed. Sometimes she was equally embarrassed when she returned from her visits to Jörg, embarrassed because once again she hadn't managed to confess to him about her life outside, just as outside she didn't confess that her feelings and thoughts revolved around him. Other times she came back stressed, because she had experienced Jörg only as a duty, and she was fed up with lying, which was unavoidable because their different lives, based on different truths, needed the bridge of lies. Then again she suffered from the helplessness she felt

with regard to Jörg, the jail, the state and her own situation, even though she was still racing around and around
in the same spot like a hamster on a wheel. No, Margarete didn't look down on any of the guests because
they had problems with Christiane's closeness to Jörg.
But she was looking forward to Sunday, when the house
would be empty again, and she would be alone.

The grass beneath Margarete's feet felt even better
than she had imagined. Its stalks were damp, slippery
and supple and invited her to slide. Once, she overdid it,
lost her balance and fell on her back, which took her
breath away for a moment. She lay there, her left side
hurt, and she laughed. At the cockiness of her footsteps
and the pride that comes before a fall. Had she been
looking down on her guests? She liked being alone, and
she was alone a lot. When she met people, she often
found them deeply strange, their behavior incomprehensible, their confidence unsettling. Was what Margarete experienced as the detachment of strangeness
really the detachment of arrogance? Her eyes drifting to
the branches and the sky, she saw the leaves trembling in
the wind, and she saw a star wandering until she realized
it was a plane. Then she heard crows, very near and very
loud. Had they spotted an enemy and wanted to drive it
away, or were they arguing? Did crows wake up at night
and argue? If they cawed any longer, they would wake
the whole house.

Margarete got to her feet and walked on. She
walked to the bench where Ilse had sat writing, and sat
down. She had set up the bench here. She had long
dreamed of a house by a lake or a river. Now bench and

stream fulfilled the dream of waterside life, and Margarete was content with it. A lake or river she would not have had to herself; the stream she did.

Sometimes she was irritated by how happy she was to withdraw. How rounded, how light, how serene life was alone. Until the escape suddenly made possible two years before the fall of the Berlin Wall, she had been different, more sociable, more open to contact, more needy of it. But she didn't feel at home in the West, and when she had the chance to return to the East, it too had become strange to her. Her work as a freelance translator put her in touch with an editor every few weeks, and if she couldn't find something on the Internet she had to do some research in the state library in Berlin, that too every few weeks, and sometimes she would fall into conversation with another user, sometimes even over a coffee. There was the shared flat with Christiane. But since there had been the shared house in the country as well, Margarete often lived alone in the garden house for weeks on end.

Was she, by withdrawing, losing her capacity to empathize with others? She had tried to go along with Christiane in her concern for Jörg, and she had also set about trying to like Jörg and help him. But even though she understood her friend's relationship with her brother after stories that went on all night, she thought it was sick and understood it only as one understands an illness. She thought Jörg was sick too. Wouldn't you have to be sick to kill people not out of passion and desperation, but with a clear head and in cold blood? Wouldn't someone healthy simply have other and better things to do? Listening to Christiane and her friends talk about the RAF and Germany's autumn of terror and the pardoning of terrorists, time and again Margarete had the sense of something sick, a subject in which people were talking about a sickness that had afflicted the terrorists back then and was now afflicting the speakers. How can a person in a healthy mental state discuss whether society is made better by showing mercy to murderers? That showed far too much respect for an ugly, repellent sickness. No, Margarete could feel only the empathy that one has for the sick. Was that too little?

The cool of morning came, and Margarete lifted her legs onto the seat, pulled the nightshirt over her feet and wrapped her arms around her knees. Soon it would be day. With the first gleam of sunlight she would get up, go back, lie down again and go back to sleep. No, the empathy that she had for Christiane and Jörg and the guests was not too little. It wasn't an almsgiving empathy, which one gives while at the same time seeking distance. She looked forward to being alone again. But now the others were there, and she wanted to do what she could to keep the sick from becoming even sicker. At peace with herself, she nodded off, and her head sank to her knees. When cold and pains awoke her, the sky was brightening in the east.

Saturday

First the sun bathes the crown of the oak in front of the house in bright light. Now the birds that live there, and that have been chattering since the break of dawn, start getting noisy. The blackbird sings so loudly and insistently that whoever is sleeping in the corner room wakes up and can't get back to sleep. The sunlight wanders down the side of the house facing the road to reach, around the back, the other oak, the garden house, the fruit trees and the stream. It shines too on the shed to the north of the garden house, which Margarete would like to turn into a henhouse with a chicken run. She would like to be woken by the crowing of a cock.

Apart from the birds the dawns are quiet. The bells of the village church don't start ringing till seven, the main road is far away and the railway line even farther. The farm co-op, whose vehicles used to set off for work in the early morning and from whose stalls the wind used to carry the mooing of the cows, ceased to exist a long time ago; its stalls and sheds are empty, and its land is leased and run by a farm in the next village. The residents of the village who have work don't have it here; they leave on Sunday evening and come back on Friday evening. On Saturday and Sunday morning they sleep late.

The dawns are quiet, and they are melancholy—like

the noontimes and evenings, like the mornings and the afternoons. They are melancholy not only in autumn and winter, but also in spring and summer. It's the melancholy of the high sky and the wide, empty land. The eye finds no purchase among the trees, the church tower, the electricity supply with its masts and cables. It finds no mountains in the distance and no city nearby, nothing to set boundaries and create a space. The eye loses itself. The visitor who lets his eye wander loses himself along with it, and it saddens him and is at the same time so compelling that he is seized by the longing to merge with it. Simply to lose himself.

Anyone who was born and bred here, and who sets about taking a job and founding a family, has to make his mind up. Stay or go. Staying small under this sky and in this void or growing at the cost of a life away from home. Even those who do not consciously make the decision sense that if they stay, their lives will be small even before they have really begun, and that if they leave, they are leaving behind not just a place but a life. A life whose small format is full of beauty—that's why the visitors come back and buy themselves a house or a farm and yield to the desire to lose during the weekend. The fact that the small format is also full of ugliness doesn't bother them. They don't suffer from the monotony, they don't feel that whatever they do they might equally well not do, they don't get tired, they don't get angry, they don't lose themselves in alcohol.

And it was ever thus. There were always those who stayed, those who left and those who lived partly in the big city and partly in the country. It was always a matter of merging or leaving, and some who could afford it always managed to enjoy the melancholy without succumbing to it. Margarete was irritated by talk of the decline of the wide, empty land between the big city and the sea. She didn't think things were better under socialism or, as far as she could tell, under the rule of the Junkers. She didn't believe political and social systems were important. The melancholy was important. It more than anything else informed the land and the people.

Margarete had grown up in a neighboring small town and had left for Berlin, planning never to return. To learn foreign languages, travel far away and stay far away. But in the end she had moved back here, at first only for the weekend, then for months at a time. She had belatedly merged with it—though not entirely, because she still had the flat with Christiane in the city. But her garden house, her bench by the stream, her rambles, her translations, her solitude—it was a version of the little life before she escaped, and she knew it. She hated melancholy when it imposed depression upon her. But mostly she loved the melancholy. She even believed it healed people. Anyone who loses himself in the high sky and the wide, empty land also loses what it is that is making him suffer. Margarete doubted whether meeting up with their friends had been a good idea. But it had certainly been right for Christiane to bring Jörg here first, after his release. Perhaps his sickness would go into remission, along with everyone else's.

Seventeen

Jörg woke before all the others. He woke with a feeling that everything was fine: his body, his state of mind, the new day. Then he gave a start—just as he had given a start in prison when he had woken with the same feeling and seen the neon lights, the bright green walls, the basin, the toilet and the small, high window. But now the walls were white, jug and basin stood on a chest of drawers and tulips on a table and fresh air came through the big window. He had given a start only out of habit. Relieved, he crossed his arms under his head and was about to make plans—just as in jail he had liked to start his days with plans for the time afterward. But now that he could not only make plans but also realize them, he found it hard. Putting Henner on the spot for his betrayal—he had done that yesterday. Why couldn't he think of anything else? He could listen to Christiane's and Marko's plans, and perhaps Karin and Ulrich and Andreas had plans for him too. But why did he have none himself?

Ilse knew what she wanted as soon as the blackbirds in the oak tree woke her up. She got out of bed, got dressed, picked up notebook and pen and crept on tip-toe down the corridor, downstairs, through the kitchen and out of the house. In the park she went to the bench by the stream. She opened the notebook and read what she had written, three short chapters in a loose sequence that wasn't right. Should she establish a connection between the chapters? She could go with Jan as he was picked up by his French colleagues in the ambulance and taken to Germany, as he was put in a deathlike state for the second time, laid out and displayed in an open coffin at the funeral. Or should she rework the chapter about Jan at the coast? Jan couldn't help cursing the swinish system, the assholes in politics and business and the fucking cops. She didn't want to write it down like that. But if she couldn't make Jan talk like a terrorist, how could she make him commit murder?

No matter how quietly Ilse had trodden, the creaking floorboards had forced their way into Karin's sleep. In her dream she was late, she wanted to creep quietly into the church where the congregation was waiting for her, but the floorboards gave her away and all heads turned toward her. She woke up. Her husband was still asleep, and she let him sleep, even though she would have liked to wake him. She prayed, or perhaps it was a meditation or a moment of truth. Was it true what she had said the previous evening? Did she see the terrorists as her confused brothers and sisters? Did she have fraternal feelings for Jörg? Did she want to have them? Did she think she had to have them?

Ingeborg too was woken by the creaking floorboards. She listened to Ilse's fading footsteps and waited to hear whether yet more footsteps would come and go. But it remained silent. She looked at the clock and nudged her husband. "Let's go, while the others are still sleeping."

He shook his head, irritable that she had woken him and wanted to creep off. She's beautiful, he thought, but if things get hard she always wants to take the easy way out. He looked at her. With her bleary face she wasn't even beautiful.

She insisted. "I don't want the others to make me look ridiculous, not me and not my daughter."

"No one wants to make you look ridiculous. The others will be incredibly considerate and emotionally gentle. And your daughter is mine too and she doesn't take the easy way out—she faces up to things."

"And what if there's another row?"

"Then there's another row."

Taking the easy way out, facing up to things—when she woke up, their daughter didn't care. The evening had been silly in the end, but she had slept well, and now it was morning. That was how it was: sometimes things worked out with people, sometimes they didn't. Life went on. Sometimes they worked out today with a man they hadn't worked out with yesterday. As to the great terrorist who had panicked in front of her, maybe she would give him another chance. Anyway, that had never happened to her before: she had made a man panic!

Marko was also concerned about Jörg's panic. How much political power could you expect from someone who panics at the sight of a naked girl? For four years Marko had been busy trying to turn Jörg, the terrorist who hadn't distanced himself from the RAF, into the intellectual head of a new terrorist movement. He had hoped Jörg would reply with a political thunderbolt, an interview, a press declaration, not illegal, but hard-hitting. He had imagined that Jörg, once free, would be full of plans and hungry for action. Instead he was tired and panicky. Four years' work for nothing?

At first Andreas had suited Marko just fine: a lawyer who could make sure that Jörg didn't cross the bounds of legality with his thunderbolt. Then they had argued. But Marko was willing to bet that if Jörg wanted to, his lawyer wouldn't hold him back.

Andreas saw things differently. He had no time for Jörg's political nonsense. He had threatened to resign his mandate if anything like that welcome address happened again. In the event of a thunderbolt after his release, he would have nothing more to do with Jörg. As a matter of fact the previous evening had been quite enough for him. Yes, the view of the sky from his bed was beautiful—at breakfast he could pull the bishop's leg, then go for a walk and look at trees. But not until Sunday!

Henner too was dreading the two days he was still supposed to be spending there. When he awoke, the conversation with Christiane had come into his mind and saddened him again. What a life! And from thinking about her life it was only a short step to thinking about his own life. Was it any better? Work was going well, and he was successful, and when he was working on an exciting report the thrill was as great as ever. But his relationships with women weren't right. They were relationships that neither began nor ended, but which he slipped into and crept away from. They were women he didn't want, but who wanted him. And although he longed for a different kind of relationship, he was incapable of meeting women any other way and seeking out the right ones instead of being found by the wrong ones. The knowledge that it had something to do with his mother didn't help. Sometimes he thought his mother's death would set him free, but he immediately doubted whether that would be the case. Work helped, even if it didn't solve the problem. But it no longer helped as much as it had, and this weekend there wasn't any work at all.

When he came into the kitchen, Christiane and Margarete were making breakfast. "Am I the first?" Margarete nodded and handed him the coffee and the grinder. Christiane cracked eggs, chopped up onions and ham, mushrooms and tomatoes and smiled briefly at him. Margarete put crockery and cutlery on a tray and carried it onto the terrace. No one spoke. Then Henner drove into the little town by the lake and fetched rolls. When he came back, the other two were sitting on the terrace drinking the first cup of coffee and the first glass of Prosecco, and he joined them. Christiane smiled at him briefly again; now he saw that it was a nervous smile. He wanted to ask her if everything was all right, if she had slept well. But when Margarete put her hand on Christiane's arm his question seemed like idle chit-chat. So they sat there in silence and looked at the park, alone with their thoughts.

Eighteen

It was ten o'clock by the time they were all gathered around the table. Dorle was last to come down. With ponytail, no lipstick and wearing a big white linen skirt and white linen blouse, she looked fresh and sweet, and she politely did the rounds of the group and greeted each one in turn with the hint of a bow. Ulrich was proud. His daughter had reinvented herself. She was in a theater group at her school; he would also send her to private acting lessons.

Jörg had only been waiting until the group was complete. "Yesterday you wanted to know all kinds of things about me—I'd also like to know something about you, or more precisely, about . . ."

Ulrich wouldn't be deterred. "But yesterday you didn't say what I wanted to know about you. What about today?"

"I didn't . . ."

"No, you didn't, and then my wife came to your aid and you escaped to bed."

"I don't remember your question, I'm sorry. Can I . . ."

"I asked about your first murder. How you felt when you were doing it. Whether you learned anything about it for life."

Ingeborg didn't get involved this time, and the others had come to terms with the fact that Ulrich wouldn't let go. Everyone looked at Jörg.

He raised his hands as if he were about to speak and emphasize his words, and then lowered them. He raised them again and lowered them again. "What should I say? In a war you shoot and kill. What are you supposed to feel? What are you supposed to learn? We were at war, so I shot and killed. Are you happy now?"

"Wasn't your first murder a woman who wouldn't give you her car? When you'd robbed a bank and had to get away?"

Jörg nodded. "She hung on to her stupid car as if it were heaven knows what. I would rather not have fired—it was the only way. And don't try to tell me the woman wasn't at war with me or I with her. You know as well as I do that it isn't just soldiers who die in war."

"Collateral damage?"

"Why the sarcasm? Tell me we waged the wrong war and I won't contradict you—we misjudged the situation. But we did wage that war, and we waged it as you wage a war. How else?"

Karin looked sadly at Jörg. "Are you sorry about it?"

"Sorry?" Jörg shrugged. "Of course I'm sorry we chased a project that came to nothing. Whether it could have come to anything—I don't know."

"I mean the victims. Do you feel sorry for the victims?"

Jörg shrugged again. "Sorry? Sometimes I think of them, of Holger and Ulrich and Ulrike and Gudrun and Andreas and . . . and all the ones who fought and died, and, yes, sometimes I also think about that woman who wouldn't give up her car, and the policeman who wanted to arrest me, and the bigwigs who stood for this state and died for it. I'm sorry that the world isn't a place where people don't . . . that it's a place where they . . . So of course no one should have to fight and die, but sadly the world isn't like that."

"The world's to blame, I understand. Why can't the stupid world be the way it's supposed to be?" Ulrich laughed. "You really are a sweetie."

"Enough of your cheap sarcasm. You have no idea what Jörg's talking about. Have the cops ever beaten you up? Have they shackled you by your hands and feet in a jail cell and left you lying in your shit and piss for two days? Have they forced food down your throat, down your windpipes and your bronchial tubes until your lung collapsed? Have they deprived you of sleep night after night for years? And then left you for years without a sound?" Marko bent over the table and yelled at Ulrich. "It really was war—Jörg hasn't worked that out. Back then you knew it too—everyone knew. How many leftists have I met who have told me they nearly ended up in the armed struggle back then! They didn't, they preferred to have other people fighting and failing for them—vicariously. I understand that people are afraid of the struggle and stay out of it. The fact that you act as if there hadn't been a war leaves me speechless."

"You, however, are quite talkative. No one goes vicariously into war for me. And vicariously shoots women who don't want to hand over their cars, or chauffeurs who have to drive company directors around. Do they for you?" Ulrich looked around.

Karin shook her head. She looked dejectedly at Jörg. She couldn't believe her ears. At the same time she worked to reconcile what he and Marko and Ulrich had said. "No, Ulrich, I haven't had anyone vicariously kill for me. But we all believed that we had to leave bourgeois society behind if we were to lead an uncorrupted life. And . . ."

"Such nonsense." Andreas snorted contemptuously. "If society doesn't suit you, you can go to a nunnery or go and raise bees in Provence or sheep in the Hebrides. That's no reason to kill people."

Karin wouldn't give up. "Would so many of us have taken the liberty of leaving or changing society if the armed struggle hadn't existed as an extreme possibility? It wasn't waged vicariously on our behalf. But it did extend the space in which we were able to act. At the same time, anyone who killed in the struggle crossed a threshold that he shouldn't have been able to cross. We must not kill. And the way you talk about it, Jörg . . . Does prison make people like that? So cold? So coarse? I'm sure you're different inside from the way you appear on the outside."

Jörg made several attempts to speak, but couldn't decide on an answer. Karin didn't want to say more, and neither did Ulrich, Marko or Andreas. But just as the others were beginning with great relief to ask one another for bread rolls and pass one another the jam and talk about weather forecasts and plans for the day, Jörg said, "I'd like Henner to tell me something, if this is a good time."

Henner smiled at Jörg. "Why so formal?"

"More coffee, anyone?" Christiane got to her feet and went and stood beside Henner.

"What does that feel like: first putting me in prison and then celebrating my release from prison with me?"

"What are you talking about?"

"You told the cops I had a cabin in the Odenwald—they had only to wait there until one day . . ."

"Ouch!" The coffee pot had slipped from Christiane's hand, and the hot coffee had poured over Henner's trousers and feet. Henner jumped up, took his napkin and tried to wipe himself down.

"Come with me." When Henner hesitated, Margarete took him by the hand and started pulling him toward the kitchen. Then she changed her mind and pulled him toward the garden house. Henner began to protest, but she just shook her head and went on pulling.

"What are you doing?"

"I'll tell you in a minute."

"Must we . . ."

"Yes, we must."

Nineteen

When Margarete and Henner were standing by the garden house, she let go of his hand.

"What now?"

"Take your trousers off and put on a pair of mine. Then we'll wash your trousers and hang them up." Henner looked skeptically at her hips and his own. Margarete laughed. "Yes, they'll be a bit big, but not very. Fat women look fatter than they really are."

He followed her into the house and looked around. The hall led from the front door straight into the kitchen. On the left he looked into a big room with a desk, swivel chair and stairs leading upward, and to the right a room with an open fireplace, sofa and armchairs. "Where can I . . ."

"Wherever you like. I'll go upstairs and fetch the trousers." With a heavy tread she climbed the stairs. He heard her opening and closing a cupboard door, and with heavy footsteps she came back down and gave him a pair of jeans. They were freshly washed and felt rough and unwieldy. He turned away and changed. She was right: the jeans were big, but with a belt they were all right.

In the kitchen she took a zinc tub out from under the sink, threw his trousers into it, screwed one end of a hose onto the tap and laid the other in the tub. She looked at the cylinder below the ceiling. "I hope I've got enough—otherwise you'll have to get out and turn on the pump." She let water flow into the tub and added a few squirts of dishwashing liquid.

"Will that clean my trousers?"

"No idea. I take my stuff to the Laundromat."

She knelt down and pummeled and kneaded the trousers until the water foamed. "What do you say we let them soak for a bit?" She tried to straighten up, but fell back to her knees with a shriek of pain. He bent down, put his arms around her and helped her up. Like a tree, the thought ran through his head, as if I were hugging a tree and lifting it up. When she got up, she smiled at him. "It's my disc. I forgot about it. It's slipped out to punish me."

Henner's arm was still around Margarete's back. When he took it away, he was embarrassed because he had left it there for so long. "Can't you have an operation?"

"Yes, but it might make it even worse." She looked at him searchingly. "What are you going to do?"

"What about?"

"About Jörg's question."

"Tell him it isn't true. I didn't put him in jail, I didn't tell the police a thing."

"Are you sure?"

He laughed. "I wouldn't forget something like that. Yes, back then I wondered what I would do if he turned up at my door one night and asked me to hide him from the police. For a long time I didn't know. Sometimes I thought one thing, sometimes another. In the end I made up my mind that I would take him in for a night and send him away the next morning. Luckily he never came."

"Let's go for a little walk." Margarete didn't wait for Henner's reaction, but set off, out of the kitchen and across the orchard to the stream. He put on his shoes, which he had taken off to change his trousers, and walked after her. When he caught up with her, she said, "May I?" and took his right arm and leaned on it. They walked slowly along the stream. Sometimes a frog jumped into the water, startled by their footsteps, sometimes the gurgling of the water grew a little louder. Where the forest didn't reach all the way to the stream, they walked in piercingly hot sunshine. Henner felt his body growing damp with sweat where Margarete leaned against him.

"Christiane told the police about the cabin in the Odenwald."

Henner stopped and looked at Margarete. "Christiane?"

"I think that was why she poured coffee over your trousers. So that you couldn't tell Jörg it wasn't you."

"But later I'll have to tell him what I didn't tell him before."

"Do you?"

"You mean . . ."

"Perhaps that's what Christiane hopes. Perhaps she wants to talk to you, and ask you to."

Henner scratched stones loose with his foot and kicked them into the stream. "What an absurd piece of playacting. The sister betrays her brother to the police. Then she wants her brother's friend to say it was him. The friend she once loved and then dumped because she didn't want to betray her brother." He looked at her. "Has Christiane told you why she betrayed Jörg?"

"She hasn't even told me she did betray him. But isn't it obvious? That she couldn't stand being so worried about him anymore? That she wanted him to be taken so much by surprise so that he couldn't shoot or be shot? It was out of fear that she betrayed him, out of love and fear."

"And where do I come in?"

She tried to read in his face whether he felt merely annoyed or harassed. He felt her gaze and smiled at her. "I really don't know. Do I owe Christiane anything? Do I have to help her because it doesn't cost me much? What does it cost me if Jörg thinks I'm a traitor?" Her face was first surprised, then scornful. He didn't see it. He went on seriously thinking and talking. "Or must I denounce Christiane by laying myself bare before him and freeing her of him?"

"Or must you help Jörg by freeing him of her?"

Henner heard the mockery in her question. "What's up?"

"Stop! You'll just tie yourself up in knots. Do what you feel—how Christiane and Jörg respond is their business. Right now you're acting as if they were a calculation you could solve."

He walked on, and she walked with him. Although he tried not to feel insulted, he did. As they stood there, she hadn't taken her arm from his. Now, when he tried to pull his arm away, she held him tight. "You can't do that. First you have to help me to a bench and then back to the house." She laughed. "You can do it under protest."

Twenty

After breakfast Ilse wanted to go on writing. She took
her notebook and pen and went to the stream, but saw
even from a distance that Margarete and Henner were
sitting on the bench. She took a broad sweep through
the forest. When she came back to the stream it was
almost twice as wide; another stream must have fed into
it in the meantime. Beneath a willow tree was a row-
boat, tied to the trunk with a long chain. Ilse sat down
in it and opened her notebook.

> *At last it was all over. The undertaker's employee*
> *whom the comrades had bribed liberated Jan from the*
> *equipment room and gave him the bag. "You have to*
> *get over the wall—the gate is shut." It was dark. Jan*
> *stumbled over gravestones, reached the wall, climbed*
> *up on one of the tombstones that were set into the wall*
> *and sat down on top. He looked onto a dimly lit road,*
> *on the far side of which were gardens, and far beyond,*
> *at the next road, houses. His new life started now. He*
> *threw the bag down and jumped after it.*

No, Ilse hadn't written much in the morning before
breakfast. But she had made a decision. She wanted to
know. Either she would manage to write about the
shooting and bombing and killing and dying, or she

would abandon the project and look for something else. And with the decision to try, the desire had awoken to do it—not just the writing, but the imagining. With a shudder, Ilse was beginning to enjoy it: the idea of the explosion hurling the car into the air, the bullet flying at the window, piercing the glass, hitting and throwing its victim against the wall, the pistol set to the back of the neck, the trigger pulled.

He walked along the road, passed several parked cars, found an elderly white Toyota, smashed the window with a stone, hot-wired the ignition and set off. It was his city; he knew his way around. When he was on the highway and swimming in the flow of traffic, he opened the bag and looked in. They had given him a German passport, a bundle of fifty-mark notes, a pistol with ammunition, a piece of paper with a date, a time and a telephone number. He was to ring at seven the next morning; he memorized the telephone number, tore the piece of paper into little scraps and let the driving wind carry them away. At a service area he parked the car at the end of the lot, took a room and asked to be woken at half past six.

He thought of the life ahead of him. A life as a fugitive without a place to go and hope to rest. But whether the fear of not waking up again after the anesthetic had exhausted his ability to frighten himself, or with the step into his new life the old fears had ceased to be so obvious, he felt light and free. At last the half-truths of his old life were over. At last he was living in the selflessness, absoluteness, uniqueness of the struggle. He was free, was in debt to no one, committed to no love, no friendship, no concern for anyone, only devotion to the cause. What happiness, what a rush of freedom!

He was woken by his alarm call, showered and at seven o'clock rang the number he had been given. At nine in the evening he was to meet a woman in the bookshop at the Munich railway station, blue coat, shoulder-length dark blond hair, big leather bag over her shoulder and Frankfurter Allgemeine Zeitung *in her hand. He had breakfast and found a truck driver to take him along and drop him off at the highway exit for Munich. By early afternoon he was in the city, bought a travel bag and a change of clothes and went to the cinema. They were showing a French film, a laconic and sentimental story about entanglement and parting. Jan came out of the cinema and phoned home from the nearest telephone booth—a low point for which he only subsequently forgave himself by saying nothing and quickly hanging up again.*

At nine in the evening he met the woman. She took him to a flat in Schwabing, a faceless room with a kitchenette and a shower. When she came out of the toilet without wig and makeup, he barely recognized her: a childlike face under brush-short hair. She told him what he had to do the next day. Then they heated up pizza in the oven. Over dinner they didn't talk— the only important thing was what was to be done, and that had been said. Jan was amazed by the excellent red wine. When it was on his tongue he

*wanted to ask the woman how she had got hold of the
bottle. After swallowing he let it go.*

*Then they lay down in bed and made love.
Memories of Ulla darted through Jan's head. "Let's
make love," she had urged him when she wanted him,
and spurred him on with "Love me" when she
wanted to come. It had been emotional, emotional and
gooey. Now Jan felt as if he and the woman were
dancing a perfect dance in bright, cold light. What
purity of pleasure, and again: what a rush of freedom!*

*They stayed in bed for a long time. That
afternoon they took the tram to the suburbs, walked
through the streets as naturally as if they were on their
way home and went past the chairman's villa. It all
looked as the woman had described it to Jan; the
garden gate and wall were not under video camera
surveillance. At the end of the property Jan climbed
into the garden, slipped to the house under the shelter
of the bushes, hid behind the rhododendron by the
front door and waited. He heard the bell ring, saw the
chairman coming along the garden path, followed by
his chauffeur with two briefcases, saw the chairman's
wife walking up to the door and greeting her husband,
saw the chauffeur going in and coming back out again.
After a while he heard the bell ring again and saw the
chairman's wife opening the door again. His
accomplice came along the garden path, waved an
envelope. As she handed it over, Jan pulled the ski
mask over his face, jumped up, pushed the chairman's
wife into the house, forced her to her knees and held
the pistol to her head. As he did so he yelled: "Don't*

*do anything stupid, don't do anything stupid!" He
yelled at her and yelled at her husband, who stopped at
the bottom of the stairs, raised placating hands and
said, "Calm down, please, calm down!" Neither
resisted as they were tied up. The woman started
crying, while her husband went on talking. When
Jan couldn't bear to hear it anymore, he took the scarf
that the woman's husband had just taken off and
stuffed it into her mouth. With horrified eyes the
husband watched his wife choking and stopped
talking. Jan led him upstairs. "The safe is in the
bedroom," said the man, and Jan led him into the
bedroom and sat him down on a chair. "Behind . . ."*

*He would have said behind which picture or
which piece of furniture or in which wardrobe behind
the clothes the safe was to be found and how it was
opened. Later Jan thought he should have looked in
the safe anyway—beginner's nervousness. He put the
pistol to the back of the man's head and fired, and as he
pulled the trigger he closed his eyes, shut them tight,
and he was shaken and he had to control himself not to
fire again and again. He opened his eyes and saw the
man sinking forward and off his chair. He couldn't
bring himself to kneel down beside him and put his
hand to his wrist. He saw the blood flowing, tapped
the man with his foot, first gently, then harder, until
he slipped from his side onto his back and directed his
eyes into the room, to the ceiling, at Jan. Jan stopped
and stared at the dead man.*

*He didn't hear the cries of the chairman's wife or
her footsteps on the stairs. He didn't hear anything*

*until the woman grabbed him by the arm. "What's
up with you? We've got to get out of here." He looked
up, looked at her and nodded. "Yes, we've got to get
out of here."*

Ilse herself felt as if she were waking up from an
anesthetic. *That is my work,* she wanted to make Jan
think with his last glance into the bedroom, and as he
passed the weeping chairman's wife he was to think it
coldly and proudly, and at the same time with a shudder
of horror. Just as she looked at her work.

Twenty-one

When Christiane had cleared up and washed the break-fast crockery and emptied the basins and filled the jugs in the rooms, she went back to the terrace. Everyone had left. Even Karin and her husband, who had helped her in the kitchen and then joined her on the terrace, had disappeared.

Christiane had made plans; for a boat trip on the nearby lake, a picnic in the park, dancing on the terrace. But, sitting alone on the terrace, she no longer had any confidence that anyone was interested in that. She was also worried about bringing everyone together again. Jörg would accuse Henner of betrayal again, and Henner—what would Henner say? What would Jörg make of it if Henner rebuffed his accusation?

She caught herself wishing Jörg back in jail. Or at least in a place where he was safe—safe from informa-tion that confused him, from contacts that seduced him, from dangers for which he was no match. Most of his years in jail had not been a bad time. At first it was bad, when the prison administration wanted to break Jörg's strength and he fought back with stubborn aggression against them by going on hunger strikes. But then the administration and Jörg learned to leave each other in peace. Jörg was almost happy. And he was never so much hers as during the years in prison.

She stepped outside the gate. Ulrich's Mercedes and Andres's Volvo were gone—all the guests could have gone off on an outing in the two big cars. Disappointed, concerned and relieved, she went into the house, picked up a lounge chair and was about to go lie on the terrace. But there was already someone there; Christiane recognized the voices of Jörg and Dorle. She set the lounge chair down, tiptoed through the room and leaned against the wall next to the open folding door.

"I was just terribly disappointed. That's why I was so horrible. I'm sorry."

At first Jörg said nothing. Christiane imagined him sobbing a few times and letting his hands rise and fall. Then he cleared his throat. "Of course I can see what a . . . a gorgeous woman you are. I just can't."

"Don't be formal—call me Dorle." She laughed softly. "Dorothea—I'm a gift from the gods. Take me. If you were with men in prison and now . . . I like that." She laughed her soft laugh again. "I like being fucked in the ass."

"I'm . . . I'm . . ." He didn't say what he was. He was weeping. He was weeping with the pitiful, halting sounds he had as a child. Christiane recognized them, and was irritated again. If her brother had to weep, it should be powerful, manly weeping. Dorle wasn't like that. "Weep, little one," she said, "weep." When he didn't stop, she went on talking. "Yes, little one, yes. It would make you weep, everything would make you weep, everything. My brave one, my sad one, my unhappy one, my little boy blue." At last Christiane was so annoyed by the comforting singsong that she wanted to intervene. Did Dorle, if she couldn't boast about sleeping with the famous terrorist, want to brag that he had wept with her and she had comforted him? But when Christiane stepped out onto the terrace, she saw Jörg and Dorle. He was sitting stiffly on his chair, eyes closed, shaken with weeping, and Dorle standing behind him bending over him, arms on his chest, rocking him. Jörg in his pain and Dorle in her attempt to comfort him looked so helpless that Christiane didn't want to intervene after all.

So she sidled off. In the corridor she collided with Marko. "I was looking for you." He grinned at her. "We've got to talk."

"Do you know where the others are?"

"The two couples and Andreas drove to a ruin. They're not staying long. But you and I don't need long either."

"Does it have to be now?"

"Yes." Marko turned around, went into the kitchen and leaned against the sink. "I've prepared a declaration that I'd like to give to the press tomorrow on Jörg's behalf. Jörg will be hesitant."

Christiane was already annoyed with herself for following Marko into the kitchen. Now she was going to have to hear about his obsessions! "I'll advise him not to. Anything else?"

He grinned at her again. "I don't know how you'd like things to be between you and Jörg in future. Are you fond of him? He's fond of you—still."

"I'm not going to talk to you about my brother."

III

"No? Not even before I talk to your brother about you? Or will I get coffee poured over me?"

Christiane shook her head wearily. "Leave me in peace."

"Will do. You make sure he lets the declaration go out. I can't stop him putting two and two together and working out that you've betrayed him if Henner rebuts the accusation. If it can only be someone from a long time ago, and if it wasn't his old friend . . . But I won't say anything." He laughed. "That business with the coffee was really stupid. Maybe Henner would have defended himself against Jörg's accusation so skillfully that he wouldn't have believed him. Sometimes truths sound like lies."

"Leave me in peace."

"The declaration has to go to the press tomorrow, and if you haven't persuaded him by tomorrow morning, I'll have to do it. And I'll persuade him by telling him what you've done." Marko suddenly looked seriously at Christiane. "What possessed you? Fear for Jörg? Better to live in prison than die in freedom? I don't get it." He shrugged. "And it doesn't matter anyway." He moved away from the sink and left the kitchen.

Can I throw Marko out of the house? Can I get Henner to take the blame for the betrayal? Can I discredit Henner in such a way that Jörg doesn't believe him? Can I get Andreas involved? Can I soften the declaration? Can I run away? Can I get Jörg to understand why I had to do what I did?

Christiane remembered giving the police the tip-off. She had given it anonymously, and that made her feel as if she had not really given it, as if the tip-off had somehow given itself. She remembered the relief she had felt when Jörg was safe in prison. She remembered the fear she had felt while he was free. It wasn't the fear that you have for someone who won't give up climbing mountains or hang gliding or driving race cars. It was a knot in Christiane's belly that tied fear and pain and guilt together. The pain of having lost Jörg already, the fear of losing him completely, the guilt of not saving him while she could have done so with a simple tip-off. With this betrayal, too, she was piling guilt upon herself. But what was that guilt compared with Jörg's life!

Then came the prison years, in which she had given Jörg everything. Christiane had thought that would let her pay the price for the guilt of betrayal. Wasn't that enough? Now she was to be deprived of Jörg's love as well? If that was how it was to be, then that was how it would be. Christiane realized with astonishment that she could think something that had previously been unthinkable without the world coming to a standstill and life coming to an end.

Twenty-two

She went to the spot in the park where her telephone worked. Previously there had been a pond here, and as always when she telephoned, Christiane wondered if the ground was still damp and that was responsible for the reception. She dreamed of repairing the channel from the stream to the hollow of the pond and from the hollow back to the stream and filling the pond again.

She called Karin. She had stopped taking pleasure in her plans, and encouraged Karin to drive to the castle by the lake, which wasn't very far away. "Take your time. I'll have an aperitif ready for six."

On the way back, through the trees she saw Margarete and Henner sitting on the bench by the stream. At first it gave her a stitch, then it sat easily with her mood of renunciation and farewell. She would be left with her work and her apartment in town and her house in the country. Her work with patients and colleagues—that was fine. But she would have liked to enjoy the apartment and house with someone, with Margarete, with Jörg, with—the thought had crossed her mind a few times since the night before—Henner.

She walked around the house and through the gate to the road. Her neighbor, the former chairman of the farming co-op, who was displaying his collection of old agricultural instruments in a big barn and a big field, and leaning on a fence hoping for visitors, spoke to her. Had the young man found her all right? He had been polite, had said hello and thank you and left. Christiane was pleased that her neighbor was speaking to her. Although she had lived here for two years, he didn't normally greet her, and as a former holder of office he was the model for other residents of the village. But when she asked if the young man had seemed like a reporter, she immediately sensed suspicion and rejection. What could there be to report from the manor house? What was actually going on this weekend? Why were so many cars parked outside the gate? She told him about the old friends whom she hadn't seen for a long time and who had finally come to visit. He made threatening hints; if something improper was going on and the reporters didn't find it, they could be pointed in the right direction.

Christiane walked on, past the dilapidated vicarage, past the church that had been under renovation for years, and would be for years to come, past the old staging post, past the village pond with the war memorial. She didn't meet anyone. As she went by the bus shelter, three boys were sitting on the plastic seats, drinking beer. They looked at Christiane in silence and scared her with their unexpected presence. Yes, she was an outsider here—it fit her mood.

She looked out for the young man her neighbor had talked about. Was he walking through the village as well? Was he asking people questions about her? Had he found out that Jörg had been pardoned and that she, his sister, lived here? She looked at the license plates of all the parked cars—a reporter would probably come from Berlin or Hamburg or Munich. Then she found her watchfulness undignified and told herself to stop it. She had also had enough of her mood of renunciation and farewell. Being cheerful was out of the question, but being sad was mixed with defiance. She wanted to be done with them, the reporters and Marko and young brats, and if the people she loved didn't want her, they could go to hell.

Her proud defiance survived until she was back on the road to her house. It wasn't long, but it was bleak: on one side the dilapidated vicarage, the rusting agricultural implements, the damaged wall of Christiane's property, on the other side, gray disused warehouses and the sheds of the farming co-op. The road wasn't paved; with every step Christiane swirled up pale dust that hung long enough above the ground to follow her like a trail. As if the cloak of the past were hanging from my shoulders, she thought as she turned around—and the fear was there again, the fear of losing Jörg, of losing Margarete and having nothing left but work. It wasn't hot, but the sun stung, and Christiane suddenly felt like hurting those who hurt her.

Dorle and Marko were sitting on the terrace. "Jörg has gone to his room to sleep. Marko is just telling me what a hero Jörg is and that the world should get to read a declaration that will finally show them as much." She smiled at Christiane, woman to woman, both knowing that men are not heroes, but little boys, or big ones at best. Then she smiled at Marko. "Can you tell me why the hero begged for mercy?"

Christiane didn't actually want to hear Marko advocating his press declaration, or have Dorle turn her into an accomplice. But then she sat down anyway.

"He didn't beg for mercy. He put in an application, the way you put in applications for leave or driver's licenses or permission to do construction. And why not?"

"Doesn't mercy mean what happened to me was actually right, but pretty please may I be spared?"

"That may be how others see it. For the revolutionary it's simply about the chance to get out and go on fighting. If the chance presents itself, he takes it. He flees, and for his flight he tricks people and lies, he fights before the court and goes from the first to the second and third authority, he puts in applications."

"What nonsense." Christiane was furious. "Jörg didn't lie before the court so that he could get out. When he was in jail he didn't make all the applications that would have made it easier for him. He was on hunger strike, more than once."

Marko nodded. "Hunger strikes are part of the revolutionary struggle. Suicide is part of the revolutionary struggle. They demonstrate to the world that the state doesn't control its prisoners, that they are not objects, but subjects. And that their struggle is selfless, if necessary self-destructive, suicidal. I didn't say the revolutionary gives everything to get out. If the struggle can be fought in jail, he fights it in jail. But the days of hunger strikes and suicides are past. The struggle must be fought outside. That's why Jörg made the application."

"Well, hmm. I think a request for mercy demonstrates to the world that the state can act and should act. That's OK too. Who gains if Jörg rots in jail?" Dorle yawned and got to her feet. "I think I'm going to have a lie-down. When does the program continue?"

"There's an aperitif at six. But I could use some help—can you come to the kitchen at five?"

Dorle nodded and left. Was she going to Jörg? Christiane didn't care. Dorle wouldn't take Jörg away from her. The danger came from Marko.

He immediately went on: "Do you understand now? Without a declaration everyone sees things as Dorle does. Jörg, whose strength they broke. Jörg, who climbed down. You can't want that to be all that's left of him! And how's he supposed to go on living with that? It would mean his whole life was nothing."

"Let that be his business. Why do you want to put him under pressure?" But as soon as she said it, she understood Marko. She saw Jörg's animated face when Marko had praised and urged him the previous night, and she heard again how eloquently Jörg had spoken about the legacy of the struggle as they walked through the park at night. At the same time she saw Jörg with his sloping shoulders, dragging gait and agitated gestures. Marko had understood that without pressure it would be a matter of chance whether Jörg decided for or against the declaration. "Can I read it?"

"Of course." Marko reached into his shirt pocket, unfolded two pages and gave them to her. She read about the revolutionary struggle in Germany, which hasn't ended, but is just beginning, which is global, like business and politics, which overcomes cultural and religious boundaries, which finds new forms of organization and uses means different from the ones used in the seventies and eighties. The text ended: "The system cannot hide behind its lies in the face of the revolution, it can be wounded, disarmed, overcome. The provocations beneath which the system reveals itself, the explosions that reveal its vulnerability, the attacks that reveal the defenselessness of those who build upon it and live off it, the attacks that spread fear and force people to think and rethink—they do not belong to yesterday. The struggle goes on."

She saw what Marko had tried to do: come up with a text that stirred people to action and offered leadership, but could also be read as mere analysis and prognosis. Was he successful? Was it legally airtight and watertight? Christiane gave the pages back to Marko. "Andreas won't do it. So find another lawyer to look at the text. For as long as he doesn't give it the green light I'll make sure that Jörg doesn't give the declaration, whatever the cost. Yes, I know it's Saturday. But if you set off now, you'll be able to find a lawyer by tomorrow."

He looked at her suspiciously. "You don't want to . . ."

" . . . kidnap Jörg or lock him away so you can't reach him tomorrow?" She laughed. "If it would help. But it doesn't, so don't worry."

"Will you tell . . ."

"I'll tell Jörg you've gone. That you drove into town and you're talking to a lawyer about a declaration you'd like to propose to him. That you'll be back tonight or tomorrow. OK?" Christiane said it in a deliberately friendly way. They both knew she had won the round.

Marko choked back his annoyance, nodded and got to his feet. "See you later, then."

Twenty-three

Henner was saying good-bye to Margarete, too: "See you later." He had led her by the arm to the bench, they had sat down on the bench and looked at the stream and he had led her back by the arm to the garden house. By the door she took her arm from his and went in; he turned around and walked away.

But after a few steps he turned back and pulled open the door that she had just closed behind her. "Margarete!" She turned around, and he took her in his arms. She hesitated for a moment, then put her arms around him as well. They didn't kiss, they said nothing, they stood and held each other. Until he started laughing and laughed louder and louder and she pushed him from her and looked quizzically at him.

"I'm happy."

She smiled. "That's nice."

He pulled her to him again. "You feel good."

"So do you."

"And you're the first woman in my life that I've kissed first." He kissed her, and again she hesitated for a moment before closing her eyes and accepting and returning his kiss.

After the kiss she asked, "The first woman?"

"Women have always kissed me first. Women I didn't want to kiss or didn't know whether I wanted to, or I did want to, but not so quickly." He laughed. "I'm doubly happy. Because you feel so good and because I've kissed you. Triply. Because the kiss was so nice."

"Come with me!" They went upstairs. The attic was a big room with chimney, cupboard and bed and a single window in the front wall. It was dark, it was hot, the air was stale. "I've got to lie down. Do you want to sit down and join me?"

She lay down on the bed in skirt and T-shirt, he sat down on the edge. He looked at her face with its brown eyes, broad nose and wide mouth and brown hair that was turning gray at the roots. She took his hand.

"Until Tuesday I was in New York at a conference on fundamentalism and terrorism. On the second evening I went out for dinner with a woman, a professor from London, and when I had taken her to her hotel and said good-bye, she took my head and kissed me on the mouth. Maybe it didn't mean anything and it was just a variation on the usual hello and good-bye kiss. But on the way to my hotel I thought about kissing for the first time in my life. Have you ever thought about kissing?"

"Mhm."

He waited, but she didn't go on. "At home my parents used to kiss me on the mouth, and I could hardly bear it. Of course they meant it nicely. But when my father and mother picked me up from the station after the holidays and kissed me on the mouth by way of greeting, I went very cold inside. Instead of closeness the kisses created distance. And if on top of that my father, who didn't take personal grooming very seriously, smelled, it made me shudder. My father's been dead for ages now. My mother lives alone—I visit her every few weeks. Every time she kisses me on the mouth by way of greeting, and she does it so . . . Why am I telling you this? Am I talking too much? Should I stop? No? She kisses me so urgently, so pressingly, so greedily—it reminds me of a vulgar girl throwing herself at a man who isn't interested.

"My parents' physicality . . . When I was a little boy, my father took me to the swimming pool once or twice, and took me into his changing room to get undressed. My father's nakedness, his soft, white flesh, his smell, his dirty underwear—it repelled me so violently that it made me feel guilty. I never saw his naked body again later on, only my mother's. Sometimes I took her to the doctor, and she got undressed and revealed her sagging, baggy skin and her crooked bones. Again I was repelled, but I also felt pity. The worst thing is when I'm at her house and she can't control her bowels and hold in her stools. They go on the bed or her clothes or, if she's in the bathroom, on the floor and walls—I don't know with what desperate movements she scatters it like that. Because she's ashamed, at first she says nothing, but then it smells and there's no hiding it and I wash off the dried-on shit. I only say kind and comforting things and I don't stop until everything's nice and clean again. But there's nothing inside me but nausea and coldness and gritted teeth. I don't have the guilty conscience that I had in the changing room with my father. I'm startled. I'm horrified by what I find within me.

"You know those stories about nurses killing their patients? They're kind and efficient not because they like the patients, but because they're gritting their teeth. They're cold. And because the effort is so great that it could only be borne with love, one day they can't bear it anymore and coldly kill their patients. And they're not the worst. Think of . . ."

"You're not killing your mother. You're just washing off her shit." Margarete sat up and ran her hand over his back.

"But the coldness is the same. When I'm walking through the streets or sitting in the café in the square, I watch the people. The way they walk, the way they hold themselves, what they express in their faces. Sometimes I see the effort they make in their posture and expression, the courage with which they meet life, the heroic effort with which they set down one foot after another, and it fills me with deep pity. But it's just sentimentality. Because I can feel such coldness toward those people that if I had a machine gun and didn't fear the unpleasantness of court and prison, I could shoot them all."

"And all that occurred to you when you thought about kissing for the first time in your life?"

"It's occurred to me since then. Some of it only here, because I want to know whether I, like Jörg . . ." He looked at her irritably, and she realized he was suddenly wondering whether she was laughing at him.

He had no reason to wonder. "I've never thought about kissing. If I did, it wouldn't lead me where it has led you. I think you're making great leaps, from washing off shit to killing people, from doing good to doing evil, from imagination to reality. All people sometimes put themselves in imaginary situations that they would avoid like the plague in reality."

"Have you never wondered, yesterday and today, how Jörg was able to kill his victims and whether you could do the same thing too? I've realized that while I can't see myself as a credible revolutionary killer, I can see myself as a cold-headed, coldhearted murderer."

Margarete shook her head and rested it against Henner's chest. When she drew away from him and sank back down on the bed, he slipped off his shoes and lay down beside her. They went to sleep like that.

Twenty-four

Several of the others were asleep as well. Jörg and Dorle in their rooms, Christiane on the lounge chair on the terrace, Ilse in the prow of the boat. Marko was on his way into town, and the two married couples and Andreas were sitting in a pub garden by the lake; enjoying the lassitude of their heads and their limbs, they ordered another bottle of wine and looked at the glitter of the sun on the water. It was hot, in the house, on the terrace, on the stream and by the lake, and the heat made people sluggish and the sluggishness made them conciliatory. At least Christiane hoped that was what would happen to everyone when, just before she went to sleep, the good feeling settled in that everything would turn out all right.

Ilse had gone to sleep because she couldn't decide whether she should let Jan go to sleep. After the murder she was able to imagine both, a completely exhausted and an insanely elated Jan, one who goes to bed and doesn't wake up until morning, and one who stays awake all night. When she woke up she decided to let him make a night of it.

But then she couldn't go on narrating Jan's everyday life, not now. His car thefts and bank robberies, his escapes, his training with the Palestinians, his discussions with the others, his caches of money and arms, his encounters with women, his holidays—she could imagine all that, she would be able to write all that. She would have to do research: Did German terrorists, when stealing cars and robbing banks, follow a particular pattern? Where were the camps where they did their training? How long were they there for, what did they learn? When did they stop talking about political strategy and only discuss the details of their attacks? Where did they go on holiday? All those questions were answerable. The one question Ilse couldn't answer was how to proceed with the murders. Taking hostages, having them around for one to two weeks, driving them from here to there, giving them food and drink, talking to them and maybe even joking with them—and then murdering them? How would you do that?

For the first few days no one exchanged a word with him. He was bound hand and foot, not so that he couldn't escape, but so that he couldn't pull the tape from his mouth and shout. The walls were thin. By day he sat on a chair in the middle of the room, by night he lay on the floor. When they took him to the toilet, they untied one of his hands; when they gave him food and drink, one of them took the tape from his mouth, while another stood ready to knock him out if he tried to shout. None of them was ever alone with him, none was ever with him unmasked.

In all that they did with him they urged him to hurry, when getting up and hobbling to the toilet, when doing his business, when hobbling back to the room, when eating and drinking. Although they urged him to chew and swallow quickly, he tried to talk to them in between. "Whatever you want to negotiate for me—I can help you," or, "Let me write to the chancellor," or, "Let me write to my wife, please!" or, "My legs hurt—could you please tie me in a different way?" or, "Please open the window." They didn't react. Even without them talking to him, he knew who they belonged to; he had seen the poster beneath which they had photographed him.

They didn't talk to him or with him. Not that they had reached an understanding not to; neither had they agreed to finish him off as soon as possible. They all had the same need to stay away from him. When Helmut, immediately after they had arrived at the apartment, cursed him as a fascist pig, a capitalist asshole, a money-fucker, the others found it embarrassing, and Maren put her arm around Helmut and led him out of the room.

In the house in the forest, to which they switched after a few days, it was all really supposed to go on like that. But what they hadn't known was that, apart from the kitchen and bathroom, the house had only one big room. "That isn't a problem," said Helmut. He fetched from the car the hood that they had pulled over his head during his abduction and when he was being transported, and pulled it over him again. But there was a problem. Even though he was bound, taped and wrapped up in a blanket, incapable of talking to them and seeing them, he was still there. He was all the more present, the more motionlessly he sat on his chair; when he stretched out his legs, craned

*his head and neck and slid back and forth, his presence
was more bearable. Because they didn't want to give
away their voices and didn't speak in front of him, it
was silent in the big room, and they heard his heavy
breathing. By day they could go into the kitchen or
outside the house. At night they couldn't escape his
breathing.*

*Then, between chewing and swallowing, he
said, "I'm not getting enough air through my nose."
He said it again and again, but they paid no
attention. Until he fell from the chair. Maren pulled
the hood from his head and the tape from his mouth,
and he breathed again. They were all unmasked, and
Maren had had the presence of mind to pull the hood
back over his head before he came around.*

*From then on they stopped putting tape over his
mouth, and sometimes he spoke. He discussed politics
with them and, because they didn't join in, he played
their part as well. He told them about himself. He
began with "You can plainly imagine, that I . . ."
and then with "actually . . ." he came to the point.
So he spoke of his time in the war, his business career,
his contacts with politics. He never spoke for more
than fifteen to twenty minutes. He was skillful; he
wanted to plant some seeds within them, to sprout and
force them to see him not as a stereotype for capital or
the system, who could be killed, but as a human
being. Then he started talking about his wife and his
children. "I couldn't have divorced my wife, however
unhappy we were together. When she died
unexpectedly, I thought that I too was dead to love and*

happiness. But then I met my current wife and fell in love again, first with her and then with our daughter. I didn't even want to have children, and wasn't even really pleased when she was born. But then . . . I fell in love with the little face that had turned toward me, with the chubby arms and legs, the cuddly belly. I fell in love with the baby the way you fall in love with a woman. Strange, isn't it?"

His voice was loud and resolute. When he spoke questioningly, hesitantly, thoughtfully, Jan said to himself, He's playing a part for us. Even when his massive form slumped in the chair or his broad, fleshy face collapsed and assumed an anxious, tearful expression, Jan thought he was playacting. The man is fighting with the means that he has. If he is freed, will he give an account in a book or an interview of how he manipulated us? Or is he so put off by the idea of showing weakness that he won't admit it, even though he did it to manipulate us?

If he is freed —they had granted an extension of the ultimatum and photographed him again beneath the poster holding up a current newspaper. If the comrades weren't released, they would have to shoot him. How could anyone take them seriously if they let him go?

For the last few days of the ultimatum it rained. It wasn't cold; they sat under the roof outside the house and looked into the rain. Scraps of fog hung in the trees on the meadow, and behind them the forest and mountains disappeared among deep clouds. Even when the door was closed they could hear what he was

*saying. And similarly he heard the news coming from
their transistor radio on the hour. When they drew
lots for who was to shoot him, they were quiet; he
wasn't supposed to hear that.*

*Jan tried to read. But he could no longer establish
a connection between what he was reading and the
way he was living. The lives he read about in novels
were so alien, so false, that he could make nothing of
them, and he couldn't make anything of books about
history or politics or society either; he had opted
against learning and for the struggle. His inability to
read caused him a small pang. It's only a pang of
leaving, he thought, one of the last; I've already put
the others behind me.*

*An hour before the ultimatum ran out the hostage
said: "When the time is past, you will act quickly—
can I write a letter to my wife?" Helmut sarcastically
repeated, "a letter to my wife." Maren shrugged. Jan
got to his feet, fetched paper and pen, took off his hood
and untied his hands. He watched him writing.*

*"My dearest, we knew I would die before you.
I'm sorry I have to go so soon, that I have to leave you
alone so soon. I'm going richly endowed; for the past
few days, when I've had so much time to think, my
heart has been full of our years together. Yes, I would
still have done lots of things with you, and I would
have liked to watch our daughter . . ."*

*He wrote slowly, and his handwriting was
childishly clumsy. Of course, thought Jan, he hasn't
written himself for years—he's dictated everything.
He dictates and commands and manipulates and*

hassles. At the same time he has a young wife and a little child and a good dog, and when he comes home from his dirty tricks, the dog jumps up on him and his daughter cries, "Daddy, daddy!" and his wife takes him in her arms and says, "You look tired—have you had a bad day?" Jan took the gun from his belt, released the safety catch and fired.

Ilse got to her feet and jumped from boat to land. No, it hadn't been hard. The first murder had been hard, even though Jan had made it easy for himself by means of a kind of intoxication. With the first murder Jan had renounced the social contract according to which we don't kill other people. What could hold him back after that?

Twenty-five

When Karin got out of the car in the driveway, a young man came up to her and asked, "Bishop?"

She studied him kindly, as she had become accustomed to doing to everyone who approached her when she was a vicar. He was tall, he had a clear face, an open expression, and with his beige trousers, light blue shirt and dark blue jacket over his arm, he made a tidy, polite impression. "Yes?"

"I'd like to ask you to put in a good word for me. You are a guest here, aren't you, and I'd like to take a walk through the house and the park. I'm writing a paper on the little manor houses around here, and happened upon this one today. I sit in archives during the week, and on the weekend I drive across the country and look at what I've been reading about. Sometimes I don't find it, but sometimes I come across something there isn't anything to read about. I haven't read anything about this house."

"I can introduce you to the owners."

"That would be kind of you. You won't remember me. Nineteen years ago, in St. Matthäi, you confirmed my friend Frank Thorsten and shook my hand when I was leaving the church."

"No, I don't remember you or your friend. You're

studying art history?" She walked up to the house and he walked along beside her.

"I've nearly finished. Forgive me, I haven't introduced myself. Gerd Schwarz."

They found Christiane in the kitchen with Ulrich's daughter. Christiane was suspicious at first, then relieved. So this was the young man who'd been looking around in the neighborhood. She instructed Karin about the state of the meat roasting in the oven and walked through the house with Gerd Schwarz. Did she know who had built the house? It reminded him of the houses built by Karl Magnus Bauerfend in the 1760s and '70s. The wide entrance hall, the stairs to the second floor made of wood rather than, as was customary at the time, stone, the two lost corner rooms that could be reached only through the drawing room—it all bore his signature. Had she checked whether the ceiling and the corners in the drawing room were painted under the white plaster? Bauerfeind had liked to have the corners painted with green foliage, and the ceiling with a light blue sky with delicate clouds. Gerd Schwarz was a good talker, and he was also a good listener. Christiane's concerns about the mildew in the walls and the worms in the wood, about the roof, the pipes, government subsidies for repair—he had an attentive and sympathetic ear for everything. In the park she showed him the dip that she wanted to fill again with water from the stream. "Where the pond was, there was also a little island." He sought and found in the middle of the dip a place that was slightly raised, and on it two stones that might once have supported a bench. He was so benignly modest about everything, and Christiane was soon so trusting that she suggested he go on looking around on his own. She had to go back into the kitchen.

He wasn't alone for long. Andreas, whom Christiane had told about Gerd Schwarz, found him and wasn't taken in by his politeness or his modesty. "Have you got a mobile phone? Can I see it?" When Gerd Schwarz, baffled, gave him the phone, Andreas put it in his pocket. "You'll get it back when you leave. We don't want people making phone calls from here."

Gerd Schwarz asked with friendly irony, "Because of the radiation?"

Andreas gave a noncommittally affirmative shrug, and remained by Gerd Schwarz's side. When they had walked the length of the park and were on their way back to the house, Jörg came out of the drawing room onto the terrace. He stopped, blinked in the late sunlight and was unmistakably the person whose picture had appeared in every newspaper and on every television channel over the past few weeks. The fact that Gerd Schwarz didn't seem to recognize him, and showed no astonishment, no curiosity, made Andreas highly suspicious. But Christiane overruled him. "Stay awhile!" Gerd Schwarz was happy to stay.

If this new guest had wormed his way in, Andreas had no hope of silencing him with threats of legal action. So if a word was spoken out of place, they had to keep him there until they could be sure he wasn't going to do any damage.

"How was your outing?" Christiane asked the two

couples and Andreas, and Ingeborg told her about the ruined monastery and the concert rehearsal that they had listened to, which had impressed them. "Then we sat by the lake and got a bit drunk and sleepy and happy, until those three started arguing. The leftist project—they got worked up about it, as if anyone today were still interested."

"No, my darling." Ulrich spoke with deliberate patience. "We know no one's still interested. We were arguing about the question of what killed off the leftist project." He turned to Andreas. "You and I can agree. It was both: disenfranchisement in the East, terrorism in the West. Both finished off the leftist project. But what you're saying, Karin . . . However lovely advances in feminism and commitment to the environment might be—the fact that we sort our rubbish and have a Christian Democrat woman chancellor has nothing to do with the leftist project."

Jörg had to control himself to let Ulrich finish. "Are you attacking me again? Was I one of the people who brought the leftist project down? The project you worked on in your dental labs, and you in your legal office? What kind of self-righteous . . ." He choked on the word *assholes* but couldn't find anything else. "The leftist project means first and foremost that man can resist the power of the state, that he can break it rather than being broken by it. We have demonstrated that with our hunger strikes and our suicides and our . . ."

"Murders. That the power of the state doesn't accomplish anything any longer is apparent in all the globally operating businesses that pay no taxes, because where it should be paying taxes it's making losses and where it's making profits it doesn't have to pay any taxes anyway. You don't need murders or terrorists to do that."

Gerd Schwarz listened with interest. If he hadn't immediately recognized Jörg, wouldn't he realize now who he was dealing with? Was it possible that he had simply heard nothing about the hype surrounding Jörg's pardon? Then Andreas reflected that the new guest, if he had recognized Jörg by now, couldn't possibly blurt it out. No grounds for suspicion, then? A harmless art historian who takes little interest in current events?

Christiane looked helplessly around at the group. In a moment Jörg would once again ask Henner what it felt like to have betrayed him back then, and to be celebrating his release now. And here it came. "You didn't answer my question. You put me in prison back then and now you're celebrating my release from prison—how does that feel?"

Henner was standing next to Margarete, not arm in arm, but hip to hip. He took a deep breath. "Yes, I thought you would use the cabin as a hiding place or a store. I once drove to the cabin and dropped off a letter there for you. Perhaps the police followed me—I wasn't aware of it. Did you find the letter?"

"A letter from you?" Jörg was confused. "No, I didn't find a letter from you. But how could I have—the cops arrested me right away. Did you mention the letter when I was sentenced and you visited me?"

"No idea. All I remember is that you didn't talk to

me, you just insulted me. As a 'half-assed dilettante'—I remember that, because I particularly disliked the 'half-assed' bit. I never worked out what it was supposed to mean."

"Back then I wasn't keen to talk to the person who'd just betrayed me. So you didn't . . ." Jörg shook his head.

"You sound disappointed. Would you rather your old friend the bourgeois dilettante had betrayed you?"

"I'd rather you'd . . . No, I wouldn't rather anything of the sort. What troubles me is the fact that . . . If the police kept you under surveillance and followed you, who didn't they keep under surveillance? When had we last seen each other? It was years before I went into hiding. You weren't really a promising contact, and even so the police . . ." Jörg didn't sound so much disappointed as suspicious.

"Second-guessing the police was never your strong point. But what do I know—perhaps another of your group brought something to the hiding place or collected something from it, and the police were following him, not me. Don't you think it's time for an aperitif?"

"Just one moment!" Ulrich raised his arms. "I brought a case of champagne to celebrate and, because there's no electricity, I put it in the stream to cool down. I'll be right back."

Christiane brought glasses, Dorle olives and cubes of cheese, Andreas and Gerd Schwarz arranged the chairs in a circle and Ilse picked thirteen daisies, one for each of them.

Jörg walked over to Henner, who was standing apart from the others with Margarete, and asked, "What was in the letter?"

"Your ex-wife had killed herself—I thought you should know."

"Oh." Jörg was still suspicious. But Henner had calculated correctly. Eva Maria had committed suicide shortly before Jörg's arrest. When Jörg had worked out that this was correct, he said, "Oh," again and walked off to one side.

"You lie very well," Margarete said to Henner. "So well that I find it weird, even if you lie only for good ends. Do you lie only for good ends?"

Henner looked sadly at Margarete. "I lied so well because back then I actually did consider driving to the cabin and dropping off a letter there. I don't know if she killed herself because of him; her parents claimed as much, but then again they had rejected Jörg from the start. At any rate, Eva Maria would have had a happier life if he hadn't become a terrorist."

"But you didn't do it."

"No. It wouldn't have helped. Admittedly I couldn't have known that at the time. But I was able to think it." He waited to see if Margarete would say anything. She looked at him with dubious tolerance. "You're right. It wasn't important enough to me. It would have been nice if it had been important enough to me, if I'd written a letter and brought it to the cabin. It would have been nice."

Twenty-six

Christiane had shed her anxiety. She was enjoying the champagne, enjoying her friends, and turned to Jörg once more with her familiar, loving attentiveness. After the champagne there was dinner, more formal and delicious than the previous evening, with a white tablecloth, her grandmother's dishes and cutlery and silver candles, with four courses and, as a highlight, Rhineland Sauerbraten, Jörg's favorite dish.

Jörg talked of the time he had spent working in the prison kitchen. "The chef had been a cook in a three-star restaurant—at least that's what he said, and we believed him—until he got fed up working late and opted for the regular working hours of public service. He had dozens of recipes stored in his computer, with calories and vitamins and minerals and who knows what else, and a program that he used to turn them into the menu for the week. The recipes were standard fare, from Königsberger Klopsen with caper sauce to Nuremberg roasted bratwurst with sauerkraut, and everyone was always complaining about the boring food. But heaven forbid that he cook anything else, anything special—then the complaints really came pouring in. And even though he knew that, the three-star chef in him sometimes came out and he would insist on serving us something Thai or Moroccan."

Karin thought that was interesting. "I feel exactly like the prisoners. The dinner dates and invitations that are part of the job, and where the food is always excellent, are torture for me. I'd much rather go out and get a currywurst and fries, sit at my desk, read the paper and shovel it down. I could do that day after day. But all kinds of things happen to me every day, so the more boring the food, the more restorative it is. Isn't food the highlight of the prison day?"

"It certainly is. But a highlight isn't necessarily the same as something exciting. The highlight represents everything that you wistfully remember and miss: the normality of life outside, your childhood, when the world was still all right, if not at your parents' house, then at your grandparents', the woman who was kind to you—food is always part of it, something constant and dependable. It's much the same with the books that are read in jail. In the prison library, I . . ."

Ilse looked at Jörg and thought of Jan. How happy Jörg was! Having an everyday conversation, having something to say, winning people's attention for his experiences and observations, here and there knowing more than the person he was talking to—it did him good. Had his longing for the everyday only grown in prison? Or had it also been dormant during the years outside the law, waiting to be awoken? Did Jan have it too?

Christiane was also struck by how changed Jörg was. No suspicion, no caution, no detachment. He involved himself in the conversation. Were his strange remarks about revolution and murder and regret only a clumsy reaction that he produced when he felt he was under attack? Was it wrong to let him deliver lectures and give interviews and appear on talk shows? Because it would lead to more attacks? And for the same reason, that press declaration, legally hedged about as it was—was it another mistake?

As if on cue, Marko appeared. She saw that he had been successful and had found a lawyer who considered the press declaration to be sound. He was so enthusiastic about his success, his project, himself, that he couldn't wait to be alone with Jörg. He had to interrupt all the others and read them what Jörg was going to give the press on Sunday.

"We've already sorted that one out," Andreas said coolly. "Jörg isn't giving a press declaration."

"I've talked to a lawyer who confirmed that Jörg won't be running any risks."

"I'm still Jörg's lawyer."

"This isn't a decision for his lawyer. It's one he has to make himself."

Jörg smarted under the subject at hand, the argument and the stares directed at him by the others. He waved his hands and said at last, "I'll have to think."

"Think?" Marko was furious. "What about your responsibility to the people who believe in you, who are waiting for you? Have you forgotten them again? Are you going to stand in front of the world as the one whose spirit was broken, the one who climbed down?"

"I don't need any lessons about my responsibility,

not from you or anyone else." But Jörg wasn't sure he had brought the unpleasant disagreement to an end, and looked over at Christiane, as if she could.

"Why do you cling to your sister? Cling to the people who want to fight with you. Who don't betray you, who need you. You . . ."

"That's enough. You're Christiane's guest," said Henner, "and if she's too polite to throw you out, I'm not. Either apologize or go."

"Leave it, Henner," said Christiane. "Marko thinks I betrayed the revolution—it's been an issue between us for ages."

"What?" Jörg's face and the tone of his voice were once again filled with suspicion and resistance. "Christiane betrayed the revolution?"

"The revolution, the revolution." Marko waved his hand. "Your sister betrayed you. She told the cops they could catch you at the cabin in the forest."

"We've done that one. No one betrayed Jörg. When I brought him a letter at the cabin, the police must have followed me."

Marko grew furious. "That's not why Christiane poured coffee over you. She was afraid you would say you didn't betray Jörg. That Jörg would put two and two together and work out that if it wasn't you, only she could have betrayed him. I know she meant well, but don't you understand, Jörg? They all mean well, but they're degrading you. They're betraying what's great about you. If you do what they tell you, then your life was nothing and you're nobody."

Confused, Jörg looked from Marko to Henner to

Christiane. Karin, who was sitting next to him that evening, put her hand on his shoulder. "Don't let them drive you mad. Marko is fighting for the press declaration, he's fighting tooth and nail. You want to think about it, and you have every right. And anyway, the press declaration isn't due out until tomorrow—or have you overruled Jörg and put it out today?" She looked seriously at Marko. He blushed and stammered and assured her that he hadn't done anything yet.

"I hope it's just my severe expression that's making you blush."

Twenty-seven

Karin went on talking. "You think Jörg is nothing if he isn't what he wanted to become? You think everyone who doesn't fulfill his hopes is nothing? Few people, in that case, are anything. I don't know anyone whose life has turned out as he dreamed it would."

"So what did you want to be? I thought when you didn't have a pope, bishop was as high as you got." Andreas couldn't help it—Karin got on his nerves.

Eberhard laughed. "Sometimes something you haven't even dreamed of falls into your lap. That doesn't alter the fact that most dreams come to nothing. I'm the oldest one here, and even I don't know anyone who has realized his dreams. It doesn't mean life is pointless; your wife can be nice even if she isn't your great passion, your house can be beautiful even if it isn't surrounded by trees, and your job can be respectable and rewarding even if it doesn't change the world. Anything can be meaningful and still not be the way you once dreamed it. No reason for disappointment, and no grounds for forcing anything to happen."

"No reason for disappointment?" Marko grimaced scornfully. "Are you trying to make everything sound lovely?"

Henner took Margarete's hand under the tablecloth and pressed it. She smiled at him and pressed his hand back. "No," she said, "no reason for disappointment. We live in exile. What we were and wanted to remain and were perhaps destined to become, we lose. Instead we find something else. Even if we think we've found what we were looking for, in truth it's something else." She pressed Henner's hand again. "I don't want to argue about words. If you think it's a reason for disappointment, I can understand that. But that's how things are. Unless . . ." Margarete smiled. "Perhaps that's what makes a terrorist. He can't bear living in exile. He wants to bomb his way to his dream of home."

"His dream . . . Jörg wasn't fighting for his dream, he was fighting for a better world."

Dorle laughed out loud. " 'Fighting for peace is like fucking for virginity,' I once read somewhere. You and your fighting!"

"I like the image. My labs and you two, the women in my life, are my exile. As a child I dreamed of being a great explorer, the first to cross a desert or a jungle, but wherever I went someone had been there before. Later I wanted to be a great lover, like Romeo with Juliet or Paolo with Francesca. That came to nothing too, but I have you and my labs—what else can a man want!" Ulrich blew his wife a kiss with his left hand, and one to his daughter with his right.

"Is this the moment of truth?" Andreas looked around at everyone. "I wanted to be the lawyer of the revolution, not the legal theorist, but a practitioner who would make revolutionary justice a reality. That came to nothing too, thank God, and I don't want to go back to the home of that dream."

"My dream came late. Or should I say: it took me a long time to realize that I was living in exile. That I didn't really want to teach, I wanted to write. That I had had enough of the students, whom I would have happily taught something if they'd wanted me to tell them anything, but they wanted nothing from me; I was always the one who wanted something from them. No, I want to get out of my exile and back to my home. I want to live with people and stories that I make up. I want to write well, but if it's only pulp in the end, that's OK too. I want to sit by the window looking out over the plain and write, from dawn till dusk, with one cat lying on the desk and the other at my feet."

My, my, that Ilse. The others were startled; they had never seen Ilse like that before. She was glowing again, not blond and pretty, but confident and burning for action. And it was infectious—the others grew more cheerful. One after the other they talked about what they had once dreamed and what exile they had been sent to and how they had been reconciled with it. Even Marko joined in; he had wanted to be a driving force, and had instead found himself in the exile of the revolutionary struggle. Jörg said nothing until the end. "The way you're talking, prison was the exile I learned to live in. But as to being reconciled—no, I'm not reconciled with it."

"OK." Ulrich tried to placate him. "Apart from being reconciled to exile, we still have the memory of our dream and our attempts to turn it into reality. Back then I hiked from the North Sea to the Mediterranean—you can laugh, but it's still two and a half thousand kilometers and it took me more than six months. I didn't manage the Sahara or the Amazon, but European hiking trail Number One wasn't bad, and I'll never forget climbing the last few kilometers of the Gotthard Pass after a damp night in the tent and then climbing down to Italy in bright sunshine."

And by saying this he opened up a round of remember-the-time to follow on the round of dreams. You remember the time we put up the tent on the way to the meeting in Grenoble and the rain washed us down the slope? The time we cooked Indian food at the meeting in Offenburg and everyone got the shits? The time Doris won the Miss University competition and read from the *Communist Manifesto*? The time Gernot, who had no interest in politics and went along to the Vietnam demonstration only because he fancied Erica, suddenly shouted, "Yanks out of the U.S.A."? Everyone remembered a harmless event or two.

They waited awhile before lighting the candles; the gloom allowed the past to slip cozily into the present, like night into day. The memories were of a time that was gone and didn't overshadow the present. But the memories were vivid, and they made the friends feel both old and young. That feeling was cozy too. When Christiane finally lit the candles and they saw one another clearly again, she was happy to see in the old faces of the others the young faces they had come across in their memories. We store our youth within us, we can go back to it and find ourselves in it, but it is past—melancholy filled their hearts, and sympathy, for one another and for themselves. Ulrich hadn't just brought a case of champagne, he'd brought a case of claret as well, and they clinked glasses to old friends and old times and watched the flickering of the candlelight in the red wine, as one watches the waves coming in on the water or the darting flames in the fireplace.

Again and again more events occurred to them. You remember the time we let rats out in Professor Ratenberg's lecture? The time we switched off the loudspeakers at the President's speech? The time we blocked the streetcar rails with chisels in protest against the fare increases? The time we hung the poster about solitary confinement from the bridge over the highway? And when the police took it down, how we sprayed the words on the concrete of the bridge? The time we borrowed road signs from the courtyard of the highway department and closed off the main road so that we could hold a demonstration? Karin remembered that one, and as she said it she laughed with embarrassment. She was a little uneasy about it, but once again she felt the thrill of the forbidden that she had felt when they broke into the courtyard of the highway department, the excitement of the atmosphere with night and rain and the flitting flashlight, the good feeling of solidarity.

"Yes," said Jörg. "That business with the road signs was a good one. We were able to use it again in our summer kidnapping."

Twenty-eight

Gerd Schwarz burst out laughing. "Remember the time, remember the time . . ." He hadn't spoken until now and the others hadn't been aware of him. No memories were expected of him, but Marko and Dorle, of whom none were expected either, had intervened with occasional amazed or derisive remarks. Gerd Schwarz had sat there in silence all evening. Now he spoke, his articulation excessively clear, his tone acrimonious.

"In the little town where I grew up, I would play cards in the pub with my friends every few weeks. One evening I learned that the five old men at the locals' table had all been in the SS. I sat down at the next table and pricked up my ears. Remember the time, remember the time—it was like that all evening. Don't you remember the time we beat up the Jews in Wilna and shot the Poles in Warsaw, obviously, but: remember the time we drank champagne in Warsaw and fucked the Polish girls in Wilna. And remember the time the barber shaved the old men with the long beards, ha-ha? You're exactly the same. What about: remember the time you shot that woman during the bank robbery? Or the policeman at the border? Or the head of the bank? Or the association president? OK, we don't know whether that one was you or someone else. How about that, Dad? Don't you want to tell your son if it was you?"

Distressed, Jörg looked at his son. "I . . ."

"Yes?"

"I don't remember."

"You don't remember? You don't remember whether you shot him or someone else did?" He laughed again. "You really don't remember, and the old men didn't remember either, that they had beaten and shot and gassed the Jews."

How had they failed to notice? The others couldn't believe it. Now they saw the resemblance between father and son, his height, his angular face, the shape of his eyes. Christiane couldn't stop staring at the young man, whom she had last seen when he was two, and all she knew about him was that his name was Ferdinand Bartholomäus, after Ferdinando Nicola Sacco and Bartolomeo Vanzetti, that he had grown up with his grandparents after his mother's suicide and that he was studying in Switzerland. Art history? Or had that been part of the trick to get himself invited into the house?

Ferdinand looked contemptuously at his father. "You don't remember—since when? When did you forget? Or repress it? Or when did amnesia come like a blow to the head and, bang, wipe it out? Or did it come immediately after he died? Or did you drink so much that you murdered him in a fog of booze? I know them all, the children of the wife and the policeman and the head of the bank and the president. They want to know what you were thinking, and the president's son finally wants to know what you did, what you all did, which of you murdered his father. Do you understand that?"

Jörg had frozen under his son's contempt. He

looked at him with eyes wide and mouth half open, unable to think, unable to speak.

"You are as incapable of truth and grief as the Nazis were. You're not one jot better—not when you murdered people who had done nothing to you, and not later on when you failed to understand what you had done. You got worked up about your parents' generation, the generation of murderers, but you turned out exactly the same. You could have known what it meant to be the child of murderers, and you became a murderer-father, my murderer-father. The way you look and speak, you don't feel even slightly sorry about what you've done. You're only sorry that things went wrong and you were caught and put in jail. You don't feel sorry for anyone else, you just feel sorry for yourself."

Jörg looked stupid as he sat there frozen. As if he didn't understand what was being said to him, only that it was terrible. It wanted to smash all his explanations and justifications, it wanted to destroy him. And he couldn't argue with his accuser. He saw no common ground on which he could meet him, on which he could defeat him. He could only hope that the terrible storm would pass. But he feared this was a false hope. That this storm would stay and only wear itself out when everything was destroyed. So he had to try to protect and defend himself. Somehow. "I don't have to listen to that. I've paid for everything."

"You're right there. You don't have to listen to anything I say. You've never listened to anything I've said. You can get up and escape to your room or into the park, and I won't come running after you. But don't tell me you've paid for everything. Not even twenty-four years for four murders? Is one life worth just six years? You haven't paid for what you did—you've forgiven yourself for it. Presumably even before you did it. But only the others can forgive you. And they don't."

It's appalling, Henner thought. The son sitting in judgment over his father. The son in the right and the father in the wrong. The son escaping into a rant, the father escaping into defiance. The son who won't admit his pain, the father who won't admit his helplessness. How is that supposed to work? What are they both supposed to do? What are we supposed to do? Karin was sitting opposite him, and he could see that she too was appalled by what was happening in front of her, and that she didn't know what was to be done either. Then she tried anyway. "I can imagine . . ."

"No, you can't imagine anything. Not what it's like when your mother or father is murdered, and not when your father is a murderer. And my father can't imagine it either. He doesn't want to imagine it. Do you think he wrote to us when my mother killed herself? Or congratulated me when I graduated from high school? Or started my studies? Do you think I've ever had a letter from my father?"

"I'm sorry. Your father simply didn't manage to write to you. He . . ."

"But I wrote to him." Jörg was worked up now. "I sent him letters and cards from prison, but they all came back, and then I gave up. I wrote to him."

"What's supposed to have been in them?"

"How should I know? It's twenty years ago. I think

I told you why I wasn't living with you, but in jail. I wrote about the oppression in the world and the struggle that we were waging, and the sacrifices we had to make. I . . . What should I have written to you?"

Ferdinand looked contemptuously at Jörg again. "I don't believe a word of it. Whatever doesn't fit with your memories you forget, and what's missing from your memories you invent. Probably your role in the murder of the president was so repellent that you can't bear the memory. And you can't bear the fact that your child doesn't interest you either—or else your friends find it so wretched that you have to make up something for them. You're . . ." Ferdinand broke off; he didn't want to say what his father was. Didn't want to say he was a pig? Didn't want to talk about other people as his father had talked? He went on: "You murdered Mother too. Not with your own hands. But you did murder her. When she fell in love with you and you made me . . . She laid down her heart and her life—she was like that, everyone who knew her says as much—and don't try to tell me you didn't know." He fought back tears. But he wouldn't show any weakness to his father and his friends. His voice didn't break. "But you'll probably tell me just that. You didn't know or don't remember what you knew. You've forgotten it. Or are you trying to tell me she couldn't have been happy with you? That you prevented even worse things by leaving her rather than staying with her?"

Then he couldn't stand it anymore; he got up and walked into the darkness of the park. After a moment's hesitation Karin got to her feet.

"Don't," said Dorle, who got up as well and went after him.

If not the famous terrorist, then at least his son, Henner thought, and was ashamed of himself. Perhaps there was more to the girl than he had guessed. He was uncomfortable about the son. The longer he had spent listening to him, the more his relentlessness reminded him of Jörg's implacability back then, and he thought about how misery passes itself on and on.

Twenty-nine

As she took her first steps into the park, the light from the candles in the drawing room still shone for Dorle. Then it was completely dark. She walked slowly on, groping to find where the thicket of branches and leaves began and where the path ran, and tried to listen for Ferdinand's footsteps. Then branches close in front of her cracked and her groping hands found Ferdinand. He hadn't got far in the dark.

"Let's go to the bench by the stream," she whispered and took his hand. "To the end of the path and then right." He said nothing, but let her take his hand. She guided him, and again and again it was fine for a few footsteps and then he stumbled or she did, and she held him or he her, then they stopped, close together, to get their bearings. Their eyes became accustomed to the dark, and when they could no longer hear the group on the terrace, their ears picked up the sounds of the forest, the song of a bird, the call of the screech owl, the rustle of the wind in the leaves. "That's a nightingale," Dorle whispered to Ferdinand when the bird started singing again.

Then they were by the stream and by the bench. It was lighter here; they saw the water flowing, the trees ending and the field beginning. A light burned in the village behind the fields. They looked at each other. "My name's Dorle," she said. "What's yours?"

"Ferdinand." They sat down.

"Would you rather be alone?"

"I don't know."

"Because you don't know me? I'm the daughter of an old friend of your father's, a friend from before he was a terrorist. I don't think they were close friends; they all just belonged to the same group. My father parted with politics early on, and became a business-man, dental laboratories, and I'm the spoiled only daughter. Last night I tried to seduce your father, but he didn't want to, and this afternoon he cried, and I com-forted him. I'm like that, I get involved in things that have nothing to do with me, and if people let me I do them good. With your father I said to myself that his pardon closed the chapter of terrorism and prison and he had to learn to live again. I didn't know his wife had committed suicide or that you existed."

"They weren't married. She hoped he would marry her, all the more when I was born. But she acted as if it didn't matter and as if she were above bourgeois affecta-tion. Until he left her. And they were never really together. He met her only a few times, because she was pretty and threw herself at him. Maybe I should tell myself that times were like that then, and forgive him for dumping her and me. But I can't do it." He laughed bitterly. "Even the President of the Republic hasn't been able to pardon him for that. Mother didn't pardon him, and I'm not going to either. And as for Mother's suicide . . ."

"But the suicide happened years after he left her. How old were you?"

"I was six, in my first year at school. After Father left her, Mother never found peace. After the woman was murdered she tried to contact the parents, and after the policeman was killed she tried to contact his widow, but the parents and the widow saw her only as the murderer's wife. Children I didn't know mocked me and beat me up in the schoolyard, and although I didn't tell Mother, she found out and started blaming everybody. She also blamed herself: because I had grown up without a father figure, because I didn't do any sport, no football or handball or basketball, because her parents were worried about her and about me. Well, OK, after Mother's death they really did have to worry about me and they took a lot of trouble, and I'm really grateful to them. But I'd rather have grown up with Mother, and most of all with Father and Mother."

"Is your whole life going to revolve around that? I know a boy who's almost paralyzed by the fact that his father is a great scientist and Nobel Prize winner. There are children of famous artists or politicians who wither away in their parents' shadow. I know gays who can do nothing with their lives because they constantly have to find their identities as gays." She didn't know if he understood what she was trying to say to him, but she didn't want to ask him. "Was your father as you had imagined him?"

He shrugged. "I thought he'd be stronger, more resolute, not so pitiful. What did you think of him?"

"You thought he was pitiful?"

"Either or. Either he stands by what he did and says it was correct and still is, or else he finds it wrong now and regrets it. I could cope with either, but not with his pathetic nonsense about having forgotten everything and paid for everything."

Dorle didn't know where to go next. The obvious thing to say was that your parents, when you grow up, are always a disappointment. Her father wasn't the hero that she had seen him as when she was a little girl either. But he was all right. And disappointed? No, she wasn't disappointed in him. Besides, she saw that Ferdinand wouldn't find it any easier to free himself of his father if he stood more strongly by his actions or if he regretted them. She sensed that in order to be free of him, he would have to make his peace with him. But how? "Do you love your grandparents?"

"I think I do. They were older, and not particularly warm—they were rather reticent. But they sent me to a good school and supported me in everything I wanted to do, piano, languages, traveling. I can't complain."

Dorle tried again. "Can you understand your father? I mean, can you try? Can you talk to him more, and to your aunt and to his friends? You find him pitiful—perhaps he himself wishes he were stronger, and it's worth finding out why he isn't."

He snorted contemptuously.

She looked at him and waited. He didn't say anything else. She took that as a good sign. "If you try, you might understand the old man who hasn't got his life in order and doesn't know how to cope with it. Murders, kidnappings and bank robberies, escape, prison, revolution came to nothing—what's the point of such a shitty life? But one's own life must have some kind of point."

She looked at him again. He showed her his profile, with the lips pressed together and the cheek muscles working, and she thought he looked delightfully masculine. He bent down, picked up a little piece of wood from the ground and started whittling it with his thumbnail. She had the feeling he liked listening to her and wanted her to go on talking. But what else was she supposed to say? "Do you still live with your grandparents?"

He took time with his answer. "Sometimes on the holidays. During term time I'm in Zurich." He went on carving. "I nearly cried before. I can't remember the last time I did that, it's so long ago. After Mother's death? I'd rather harm myself than cry in front of him. It wasn't grief, but rage—I didn't know it could hurt just as much as pain. He's sitting opposite me, his belly hanging over his trousers, his puny arms sticking out of his shirt, his face collapsed, his eyes vague and unsteady, and I'm thinking, What kinds of things has this pipsqueak done? and the rage ties a knot in my chest. You think I should understand him. I often thought I should shoot him." He stood up and rested his arms on the back of the bench. "Was it right or wrong to come here?"

"Right."

He shrugged.

"It's getting chilly," she said and snuggled up against him.

He didn't pull away, but that was all. She remembered Jörg, when she hugged him, sitting stiffly on the chair, and laughed quietly. Like father, like son. But then Ferdinand put his arm around her after all.

Thirty

After Ferdinand and Dorle had left the table, Jörg stayed sitting only long enough to summon the strength to get to his feet, get up and leave. He had the feeling he had to explain himself to the others, and he started a few times but didn't know what to say. The others were dumbstruck too. They looked into the candlelight and into the darkness of the park, and when their eyes met, they smiled with embarrassment. "Good night" was all that Jörg managed as he left, and more than "good night" they couldn't reply. A little later Christiane got up as well, to follow Jörg, and this time Ulrich didn't look mocking, but nodded.

"I'll ring the bell for a little prayer meeting at nine tomorrow," said Karin, before Christiane disappeared. "Not that I would expect you all to come, just so that you'll know why it's ringing."

That broke the spell. She's relentless, Andreas thought, shaking his head, and Marko immediately announced that he wouldn't come. Ilse was also startled by Karin's announcement, but then thought that the ritual of an occasional prayer meeting was more natural than Karin's constant attempts to defuse conflicts and create harmony. Ingeborg said, "Oh, how lovely—we'd be delighted," and Ulrich was pleased to be able to look scornful again. During the announcement of time and bell ringing, Margarete was thinking about breakfast, crockery and washing up. "Who's going to help me afterward?" Everyone was ready, and why not right away, and why not the last glass of wine afterward?

When they were sitting together on the terrace again, Eberhard said, "We'll have to leave in the early afternoon. Karin's going to offer Jörg a job in her archive. Can any of you think what we could do to make things easier for Jörg and Christiane?"

"I've already told him he can work in my labs."

"If he wants to write, I'm happy to help him get published."

Marko began with the words "Well, I think . . ." and was interrupted by Andreas.

"Yes, we know you think we should leave him in peace to get on with the revolution again, the only thing he wanted to do and, if you like, did with a certain amount of success. Forget the revolution. But leaving him in peace—you're right about that. Jörg knows we can help him get a job, and he'll ask us if he needs us. You leave him in peace as well."

"Enough of that supercilious talk. You can't tell me what to do and what not to do, and you can't tell Jörg either. You're acting as if you know Jörg better than I do, but all you know is the accused, sentenced, imprisoned, weak Jörg. I know another one. You betrayed the dream of the revolution—you've all betrayed the dream and let yourselves be bought and corrupted. Not me and not Jörg. You're not going to turn him into a traitor." At first the others couldn't understand why Marko always talked himself into a rage. Until he said, "You won't be able to take it away from him anymore—I issued the press declaration today." Marko had been trying to talk himself into being right.

Andreas looked at Marko wearily, with a hint of revulsion. He got up and asked the group: "Where's the place in the park where you can use your phone?"

Margarete got up as well. "Come with me!"

Marko struck his hand on the table. "Are you mad? You want to shatter Jörg's life without even talking to him?" He jumped up, reached Andreas in one, two leaps, knocked the phone out of his hand, bent down, grabbed it, stood up and threw it into the park. Skipping with triumph like a boxer, he came back to face Andreas. Andreas turned to Karin's husband and asked wearily, "Can I have yours?" Eberhard nodded, took the phone out of his pocket and gave it to Andreas. Again Marko pursued Andreas as he left. But this time Ilse stretched out her leg and Marko stumbled and landed on the floor together with Margarete's empty chair so noisily that Ilse threw her hand to her mouth with a little gasp of horror.

For a moment they all held their breath. Then Marko sat up awkwardly. He couldn't get to his feet, and rested his back against Ilse's chair. Andreas and Margarete went into the park. Ulrich said to his wife, "Look, it's pretty late. I've had enough for today. You too?" She held out her hand, and both nodded to the others and left. Karin looked quizzically at her husband. He nodded too and got to his feet, and she did likewise. But then she stood there indecisively, until Henner said, "Off you go!" and Ilse added, "Yes, go to bed!"

Marko said, in a baffled voice, "I tripped." He held his head in both hands.

Ilse stroked his hair. "I stuck my leg out."

"Really?"

"Really."

"I was having an argument."

"You were having an argument with Andreas. And when Andreas comes back, you should go to bed. We don't want any more drama; we've had enough for one day. Henner will help you to your room. Do you have any aspirin? No? I'll bring you some when I go to bed."

Ilse sat alone on the terrace for a while. Then Henner came back and told her that Marko had gone right off to sleep; he might be suffering from a slight concussion. Andreas and Margarete asked about Marko when they returned from the darkness of the park to the light of the terrace. Andreas had been half successful. "The agencies have taken out the report about the press declaration. But it was in there for a few hours. Some newspapers will carry it, and I'll be able to get a correction out of them, but it's still awkward."

"Have we any wine left?"

"Ulrich's claret is next to the door."

There was one bottle left. They filled their glasses and clinked them again. "To the end of the curse," said Margarete.

"To the end of the curse," the others repeated.

"What curse?" Andreas asked after a while.

"Isn't it a curse, what's being passed on from the generation before Jörg to Jörg and from Jörg to his son? It seems like one to me." Margarete saw Andreas's skeptical expression and smiled at him. "We're a bit back-ward here. The ghosts still come to us in the autumn with the fog, and when cries are heard in summer it isn't just the screech owls. We still have witches and fairies, and there are curses that are sometimes lifted from us only after generations." She got up and the others went with her, and she hugged Andreas and Ilse and said to Henner, "Will you take me home?"

Thirty-one

When Christiane followed Jörg into the room, he was sitting on the bed and staring at the floor. She sat down next to him and took his hands in hers.

"Do you think my son will still be here tomorrow?"

"Would you like that?"

"I don't know. I didn't know everything would get so difficult. One would think I'd have been able to think thoroughly about everything, and I have thought thoroughly about everything. But it's like with swimming—do you remember? As a boy I spent a whole summer lying on my belly on the chair and practiced swimming motions, and when I got into the water, with the motions I had practiced correctly, I went under. In prison I was lying on the chair, now I'm in the water."

"But one day you could swim—do you remember how that happened?"

"Do I! In the autumn we went to the Lago Maggiore in the Ticino with Aunt Klara, and you swam in the lake with me, and it worked."

"You'll practice here with your friends for a weekend, and when we go into town it'll work."

"No." He shook his head. "I have to do it tomorrow, if that isn't already too late."

"Maybe the weekend was a mistake—I'm sorry. I—"

"No, Christiane, what I'm bumping into, and injuring myself as I do so, are my own boundaries. I have to drag myself out of the bog by my own bootlaces." He rested his forehead against her shoulder for a moment. "There are lots of things I really can't remember. I can't remember who fired the gun. I can't remember whether I was supposed to meet Jan in Amsterdam and left him in the lurch. I can't remember what the Palestinian woman who trained us was called, or if there was anything between us. I can't remember what I did over all those years in prison—I must have done something, but it's gone."

"We can't store everything in our memory."

"I know that too. But I feel as if things have broken out of my memory, not old, unimportant things that have to sink to the bottom so that new things have room, but parts of me. How can I trust myself?"

"Take your time, Kiddo, take your time."

He laughed. "We've never been able to do that, Tia. Take our time, let things run, take life as it comes, lie back and enjoy it—we've never learned to do that."

"The English have a saying about old dogs learning new tricks."

"No, Tia. You *can't* teach an old dog new tricks— it's the opposite."

They both fell silent. Christiane realized that she was less frightened than she had been the previous evening. She was surprised by that; none of yesterday's problems had been solved, and neither had today's. Why was she less worried about them?

She could hear from Jörg's breathing that he had gone to sleep. He was sitting on the bed, slumped, bent forward, hands in his lap. She pushed him gently, and he sank sideways onto the bed. She took off his shoes, lifted up his legs, pulled the sheet out from under him and spread it over him. Then she stood by the bed for a while, watching her brother sleeping and hearing the first drops of rain turn into an even rustle.

She saw everything in her sleeping brother: his seriousness, his good intentions, his eagerness, his lack of detachment—from everything and also from himself, his narrowness, his hubris, his recklessness, his helplessness. Would she have learned to like him if he had met her by chance? He was her brother, the one she had brought up and tended to and looked after. He was her fate, no matter what. She went quietly to her room.

Everyone was finally asleep. Andreas, after he had walked back and forth in his room for another quarter of an hour, and got annoyed again and calmed down once more and run through legal options all over again. Ilse, after she had considered and rejected the idea of going on writing, and decided to go back to the bench by the stream in the early morning.

Dorle and Ferdinand had left the bench when the terrace was already empty and dark. It had started raining, and at first it was a mild summer rain that enfolded the two of them like light, warm breath. Then the rain grew colder, Dorle shivered and they went into the house. "I haven't got a room," whispered Ferdinand, and Dorle whispered back, "You come with me." He stopped on the stairs. "I'm . . . I've never . . ." Dorle took his head in both hands and kissed him. She laughed quietly. "I have."

Ulrich and his wife heard their daughter going into her room with Ferdinand and the two of them making love. "Shouldn't we . . ."—"No, we shouldn't," said Ulrich and held his wife in his arms until the rustle of the rain reached their hearts. Then they too made love.

Karin lay awake, heard her husband's breathing and thought of the prayer meeting the following morning. Scheduling it had been a reflex, learned at countless confirmation weekends, retreats and away days, meetings and synods. But she couldn't give her friends something drilled. Every word had to be right. She could say only what she really knew. But what did she know? She knew she couldn't have stuck her leg out and tripped Marko as Ilse had done, and she was ashamed.

Margarete and Henner went to sleep the most happily. They were happy because nothing about the other disturbed them, annoyed them. That's something one might overlook if it happens in the days and weeks of falling in love, but if it doesn't happen at all . . . They were happy because they liked everything they had learned about each other. It wasn't much; she hadn't talked much about her translations or he about his reports, they hadn't introduced their families or friends, or their favorite books and films. But Margarete had liked the way he had helped Christiane, and he had liked the mixture of doubt and concern with which she had looked at him afterward. They were happy because they liked smelling and tasting and feeling each other so much. They lay naked in Margarete's bed and enjoyed the fact that their bodies liked each other, that they didn't do it independently of their hearts, but that it was a liking of their own, a treasure of their own. They didn't hear the rain through the open window, but on the roof above them. They fell asleep in a house of rain.

Thirty-two

The rain drenched the sandy ground, collected in rivulets and puddles, washed away everything that wasn't level, settled in the courtyard, flowed into the cellar. It did the plants good. For a long time the summer had been dry, and everything was withering, the hydrangeas around the courtyard gate and outside the front door, the raspberries and tomatoes beside the garden house, even the oaks, whose leaves had lost their freshness and color. When Margarete woke up in the middle of the night and heard the rustling of the rain, louder than when she had gone to sleep, it seemed, she looked forward to the hydrangeas, which would blossom brighter the following morning, the ripe fullness of the raspberries and tomatoes, the radiant stateliness of the oaks. She went to sleep again, woke up again, and the rain was still rustling outside the windows and on the roof.

That too is part of this land. That the rain from low gray clouds covers it, that the drops fall in thin trails like the ones in Japanese drawings, that the ground grows wet and heavy and sticks to the shoes. That the rain won't stop and only your intelligence saves you from the fear that a great deluge is going to pour over the land. Because that's what the rain feels like: a deluge that will end only when everything is under water.

Margarete knew the water would penetrate the cellar, that it would get into the attic through the rusty corrugated iron and, if the stream backed up and swelled between the two houses, into the kitchen. The first time these little disasters had happened, when the next big rain came, Margarete had tried to secure the place with sandbags and sheets of plastic. It hadn't done much good. She still had to bail out the cellar and swab out the attic. One day she and Christiane might have the money to build drains around the house and mend the roof. If they never did, Margarete was fine about that too. The flood was part of the land she loved. And for Margarete, love of the land included a willingness to yield to whatever it brought: cold, heat, melancholy, drought, flooding.

Margarete turned onto her side, back to back, bottom to bottom with Henner. She couldn't work out why their lying together like this was so calming, but it was. How would things go from here? He sometimes at her place in the country, she sometimes at his in town, and sometimes traveling together? She herself didn't know how she wanted it to be. She loved her freedom and solitude. At the same time that small closeness to Henner had awoken a longing for togetherness that she hadn't known still lurked within her. But she wouldn't move to the city. She wouldn't leave the country.

She listened to the rustling of the rain. Memories arose. The night in the cabin in the field, when she had run away from home at the age of seven and was caught in the rain and wasn't yet sure that the rain wouldn't flood everything and wash it away. The summer spent harvesting, day in and day out, digging potatoes out of the mud and cleaning them. The Saturday when her best friend got married and they had to put planks over the big deep puddle in front of the door to the register office before the mayor, the bride and groom and the guests could get in. The depressions she had fallen into when the rain refused to stop.

Then she counted through how many buckets there were in the house. Five? Six? Once the rain was over, they would form a chain and bail out the cellar. Marko would pass the bucket to Andreas, Andreas to Ilse, Ilse to Jörg—smiling, she went back to sleep.

Sunday

Ilse slept shallowly, woke often and was wide awake at dawn. She walked to the window and saw the court-yard, oak tree and barn wrapped in a veil of rain. Writing on the bench by the stream was out of the question. She took the jug and basin off the table and pushed the table and chair to the window. It was just light enough to write.

Ilse didn't know where it had come from over the past few days, the certainty that she wanted to write. Had it formed secretly during the months when she had played with the idea of writing? Was it a defiant response to the uncertainty that she thought she sensed in the others? Was it the result of her horror about Jörg, who had lived a false life for high stakes, only to end up standing there empty-handed? Be that as it may, she had her certainty.

At the same time she was uncertain about how to go on telling Jan's story and take it to its conclusion. She could use his story to tell the familiar tale of terrorism in Germany—she would have to do some research into that, in any case. She could also tell something she couldn't research, but had to fantasize: the story of the murders that hadn't yet been cleared up, the terrorists who hadn't been caught. Either way—how was she to conclude her story? Does Jan get caught? Does he get shot? Does he blow himself up while assembling a bomb? Does he sit out his time in prison? Does he get himself released? Does he break out? No—then the old story just goes on. He has to sit out his time. But what's that like for him? Does he feel like a prisoner of the war he's been waging? Does he feel like a victim? Is he defiant? Does he have regrets?

What do we want our terrorists to be like? Ilse had to make up her mind about how a person is really supposed to deal with his past as a terrorist. She understood the demand that the terrorist should provide clarification and show remorse. The victims' relatives want to know what happened, and society needs a sign that the terrorist wants to rejoin the social contract. Nonetheless, she had been moved when Jörg had proudly and defiantly applied for a pardon.

Or was that not the case? Could it be that she had been moved not by the Jörg who had applied for a pardon, but the proud and defiant young man she remembered? The one she had been in love with as a girl? Had she been moved only by her memory of her love?

Strange—since Friday she hadn't thought once about her love for him, let alone felt a hint of it. He had become an object of curiosity to her, one that she looked at with cold eyes and found sometimes surprising, sometimes disconcerting, always interesting. She performed an experiment on herself and remembered the morning many years before, when Jörg had come into the auditorium. As always she was sitting in the fifth row, close enough to the professor to be able to pay attention, far enough away not to be called upon to speak. The lecture on American history had just begun, and Jörg plainly wasn't one of the usual listeners. After closing the door, he stopped, looked around, studied the professor and the students, at last walked slowly to the front and sat down in the front row. The confidence with which he did that, light-years away from Ilse's inhibitions, and his cheerful, defiant face and his slim figure in jeans and a blue shirt over a white T-shirt—she fell in love with him. When he got to his feet and demanded a discussion of American imperialism and colonialism, she found brave and vivid what she would've otherwise found annoying. With a few others she ran after him at the end of the event, and thus became acquainted with his group and with politics. She clearly remembered how overwhelmed she had been by her feeling for Jörg, how helpless she was and with what stubbornness she tried to be near him, careless of how she might come across, and without any hope of conquering him for herself. Yes, the girl she had been back then touched Ilse, and she was also touched by the boy who would soon lose his cheerfulness and retain only his defiance. But it touched her only because her love had begun with the perception of his cheerfulness.

Had writing, first in her imagination and then in reality, made her cold? Or had she found her way to writing because she had become cold? Because she had stopped loving? Had she forgotten how to do it? Had she made the cats her companions because she could reflect herself in them as she could in her memory?

Ilse felt uncomfortable. She had to find out why she had stayed cold where she could have been moved, and whether she had forgotten how to love. She couldn't possibly be indifferent about it. But she was indifferent. Yes, she needed to find out. But not right now. Right now the story was pressing. How was she to bring it to its conclusion?

If it wasn't the fact of being moved by the proud and defiant Jörg who had applied for a pardon, what was it in her that resisted an enlightened, remorseful Jan in prison, one who was willing to tell all? She didn't think him plausible. She didn't think it possible that someone could drop out of a bourgeois existence with a wife and children and a good job and social recognition and become a terrorist, before returning purified to a life of bourgeois values after years in prison. However, neither did she think it plausible that someone could cling forlornly to the terrorist project in and after jail. What was left after prison?

Ilse suddenly understood Jörg's inner turmoil. But she didn't want to write about a conflicted Jan. Which meant that Jan couldn't be arrested, sit out his time in jail and be released.

Ilse looked out of the window into the rain. How does a terrorist's life end if it isn't stopped by police and court and prison? In retirement? With an American passport and a Swiss bank account? In a house in the country? Traveling, in a hotel? With a woman? Alone? Ilse had never yearned for faraway journeys and distant lands, and holidays in the Odenwald or by Lake Constance or on an island in Friesland had always been enough for her. Now she would have liked to know more about the world and send Jan somewhere far away, make him take part in a revolution and die in an attack—an attack in which his life would reveal its truth.

Ilse heard floorboards creaking in the next room. She looked at the clock; it was six o'clock, but it wasn't getting light outside, and the dark sky indicated that it was going to go on raining for a long time. Sometimes the raindrops rattled against the house, then ran down the pane. The water forced its way between the new window frame and the masonry and gathered on the windowsill. Ilse pushed the table aside, took off her nightgown, opened the window and offered her face and breasts and arms to the rain. She wished she could run out of the room and out of the house, naked, across the terrace to the park, she wished she could feel the wet grass under her feet and the wet leaves of the bushes on her body, she wished she could jump into the stream and dive below the surface. But she didn't dare. Then she imagined the slow stream turning into rapids, imagined herself heedlessly jumping in anyway, pulled along and dragged below. She was frightened.

She closed the window, got dressed and put the table back. She opened her notebook, picked up her pen and wrote.

Thirty-four

The maître d' let Jan in, but showed him to a place at the bar rather than a table. "When Mr. Barnett comes I'll call you." Jan deposited his bag in the cloakroom and sat down.

Even from his seat at the bar he could look through the window at the city, the skyscrapers, streets in between, the rivers and the bridges, behind them the large carpet of little houses, in the distance the Ferris wheel and the airport tower. On the horizon the sea glittered in the sun. The sky was a radiant blue.

Jan was supposed to deposit the bag in the cloakroom. That was all. A favor asked of him by a Lebanese acquaintance, who had also done him various favors. "If you want to go to Windows on the World in the morning, you have to be a member of the club. You can do that more easily than I can." The acquaintance smiled. Jan weighed the bag with his hand; it was heavy. The acquaintance smiled again. "It isn't a bomb."

"What do I do with the cloakroom ticket?"

"We'll call you."

Jan drank coffee. He had performed his task and could pay and leave. He had only to make sure no one spotted him leaving and brought him the bag.

The view from the window gripped him. All

*those houses, all those people, all those lives. The
energy with which people drove back and forth and
worked and built. With which they owned and shaped
and inhabited the earth. And they wanted it to be
beautiful. Sometimes they built the tip of a skyscraper
like a temple and a bridge like a harp and buried the
dead in a green garden by the river. Jan was
astonished. Everything looked right. But he was so far
away from it that he didn't feel it was right. He
remembered the fairy tale about the giant toy. In the
picture in the storybook the giant's daughter picked up
a plow, from which the horse dangled in its harness,
and the farmer from the reins.*

*He ordered another coffee and a glass of water. He
would stay in the city throughout the day, board a
plane in the evening and be in Germany the next
morning. Every time he felt the temptation to drive to
his wife's house, hide and secretly see his sons. The
university was on holiday, and his sons might be at
home. Every time he resisted the temptation. He
knew the address and phone number. He allowed
himself no more contact than that.*

*He hears the noise before the other guests look up
from their breakfast and their conversations. Loud,
dull, grinding, sucking. As if a huge threshing
machine were dragging the whole building into its
maw and shredding it. In the window the city is
crooked, crockery crashes to the floor and shatters,
people scream and hold on to the walls, to the
furniture, to one another. Jan clings to the bar. The
walls creak and groan. The city straightens up and*

sags again, to the left, to the right, to the left. A few
times the tower swings back and forth. Then it stops.

For a moment it is utterly quiet in the restaurant.
Even Jan doesn't move. When a telephone rings into
the silence, he holds his breath before bursting out
laughing with all the others. The tower is standing,
the phone is ringing, the city is unharmed and the sun
is shining. But the relief lasts only a moment. The
waiters and waitresses who want to come swarming
out to straighten the tables and chairs, the guests who
are reaching for napkins to wipe the spilled coffee and
orange juice from suits and dresses, see gray smoke
outside the windows and stiffen.

This time the stiffness does not dissolve into
laughter. The guests dash to the window, push their
way to the door, into the corridor, to the elevators.
Chairs tip over, broken crockery crunches underfoot.
The maître d', phone to his ear, assures the guests that
he has informed the fire department. Jan looks for his
bag in the cloakroom—has someone put a bomb
downstairs and is the next one in his bag? In his bag
there is a radio. People are calling one another to say a
plane has crashed into the tower, and Jan wonders
whether the radio guided the plane. The elevators
aren't there yet—you don't usually have to wait so
long for them—someone asks about the stairs, but
how are you supposed to get down 106 stories on foot;
someone fetches a meat cleaver from the kitchen, forces
it between the doors of an elevator shaft, others pull
and shove the doors aside. They look into the shaft and
see smoke and flames and the rocking cable of the

elevator. They go to the next shaft and the third and
see the same thing.

The first people are already on the stairs. The
people from the restaurant join a crowd of people from
a conference and the staff, and in the stairwells on
every floor they are joined by still others. No one
pushes—they all act as quickly as they can and help
the others who can't go so fast. The only sound is feet
on the stairs; no one feels like saying anything
superfluous, and what would not be superfluous in
this situation? Until the first group of them cough and
come to a standstill and halt the descent. Jan is one of
them; he too coughs and comes to a standstill. When
the man next to him holds his handkerchief in front of
his mouth and walks into the smoke and heat, Jan
goes with him. They don't get far. After half a step it
takes their breath away.

"How far have we come?"

"Six, seven, eight floors—I don't know."

They go back, and everyone turns around. But
their ascent soon falters as well. From above they hear
that the other stairwells are also blocked. "Onto the
roof! Let's wait for the helicopters."

Jan stays behind. He doesn't feel good and sits
down on a step. The clatter of feet fades away, but the
fire is getting noisier, and the smoke is rising higher.
Jan stands up, opens the door leading onto that floor
and looks into a hall with open doors. He goes from
door to door, from office to office; he doesn't know why
he is doing it and why he is staying here. He knows
he has to get onto the roof—soon he will run away.

He doesn't run away. He walks into an office, walks between partition walls and desks to the window, and sees that the other tower is burning as well. He nods. He wouldn't have thought the Arabs were up to it.

He hears a quiet knocking and calling and follows it to a door. He tries to open it, it jams, he pulls on the handle, pulls the handle off, kicks the door in. It's a windowless photocopy room in which a young woman is blinking distractedly. She only heard the noise and felt the impact, then the light went out, and the tower swayed, the door jammed. She has no idea what has happened. She thinks she has finally been rescued. Jan takes her by the hand, starts running, pulls her with him. When he opens the door to the first stairwell, the heat and smoke are so powerful that he immediately closes it again. He runs to the other doors, she, holding his hand, asks desperately, What's happened, why is it burning, who are you? The other stairwells are nothing but smoke and heat as well.

Jan walks to the window with the young woman and shows her the other tower. She asks, "How will they get us out of here?" He doesn't know what to say. "Do they know we're here? Have you called?" She sees his hopeless face. "You haven't called!" She fumbles for her phone in her pocket, dials 911, gives details of the floor and the office, the smoke and the heat in the stairwell. "So," she says, "what now?" He feels the floor heating up beneath his feet. The air in the room is sticky and tastes of smoke and chemicals. Jan takes a metal wastepaper basket and smashes it against the window, first with its bottom, then with a corner, and the glass splinters and breaks. He knocks the rest of the window out of the frame.

"The floor's getting hot." She lifts one foot, then the other and gives an embarrassed laugh. He nods. "We'll have to push a table to the window." When they do, the floor is already so hot that they hurry— they hop comically from one foot to the other.

The young woman also knows that the heat will reach the table they are now standing on. "What will we do then?"

"We'll jump."

She looks at him and wonders if he's being serious or if he's joking. She realizes that he's being serious. "But . . ."

"They've stretched out huge canopies. You just have to take care you don't land on your head."

She leans out the window and looks down. "I can't see anything."

"You can't see anything. Modern canopies are made of transparent synthetic material."

She looks at him, doesn't believe him, starts crying. "We're going to die, I know it, we're going to die."

"We'll fly. We'll take each other by the hand and fly into the morning."

But even that doesn't help. She cries, she shakes, as he takes her in his arms and tries to calm her she pushes him back; she wants to go home, she wants her mother, she fumbles for her phone again, gets the answering machine and leaves a message that she loves her mother. Jan listens and wonders whether he should say good-bye to his wife and children, one first and last call home. But the moment quickly passes. He isn't going to get sentimental just before he dies. He wants to help the young woman. Like the orchestra on the Titanic.

The floor covering softens, and the table legs sink into it, not all at the same time, not all equally deep. The table tips over and stands at an angle. The young woman loses her balances, cries out, tries to hold on, but misses Jan, a partition wall, the window frame, her arms reach into the void. She tumbles out of the window and falls, flails her arms around, pedals with her legs. Jan struggles, but keeps his balance.

He has to jump. The table is getting warm, it will soon be hot, it will burn, flames are licking at various spots in the floor. Jan knows he won't scream and wave and pedal. But he doesn't want to tense his muscles and clench his teeth. He wants to fly. He wants not to be afraid of the quick, brusque, painless end and enjoy the flight. He always wanted to be free, he has slipped all bonds, he has lived in the light of freedom and with its terror. Everything he has done was right, if he flies now.

Jan jumps and spreads his arms.

Thirty-five

At nine Karin rang the bell. She didn't expect many people to come. She even hoped no one would come and the prayer meeting would be canceled. She had planned to read the verse about the truth making you free, and add a few thoughts about living in truth and the lies of life. But the dreams she had woken with several times irritated her. She had dreamed of the embryo that she had aborted as a young woman, of her husband sitting on a bench and smiling, wobbling his head and not recognizing her, about her former congregation consisting of artificial people, as low-maintenance as the Stepford wives. Her dreams were trying to warn her of lies about a life lived in truth. But why? She hadn't planned to demand a life lived in truth and condemn life lies. She had never told her husband about her abortion.

She would have if he had asked. But he hadn't asked, not even when it turned out that they couldn't have children and the fault was on her side. Sometimes she thought he guessed; he knew that she had wild years behind her, and wasn't happy about some of the things she had done back then, and perhaps he wasn't asking out of love. Was she supposed to devalue that silence born of love by confessing?

Karin went into the big room, opened the doors, let the air in, stood in the doorway and looked into the park and the rain. She breathed in the cool and damp, forgot for a moment her worries about the prayer meeting and felt beautiful and strong. She enjoyed her strength. She was a disciplined, resilient worker; when others were stressed and excitable she introduced peace and structure and made plans and decisions with a light, safe hand. She was good in her office; she taught her church to live with fewer taxes and fewer believers, when she spoke publicly about the issues of the day she found the right tone and when people sought her advice she looked them in the eye with concern and sympathy. Sometimes she suspected her heart was no longer in it and she enjoyed her job only because she did it well. But should she give it up for that reason? She also enjoyed the fact that she was a beautiful woman. She was slim, she had big brown eyes and a smooth, taut face, which was lent a fashionable finesse by her gray pageboy cut. Even when she frowned she looked younger than her age. When she lost herself in her thoughts and dreams or concentrated as she played the violin or the guitar, her eyes had a gleam that wasn't childlike and yet, like a child's beaming smile, it was a gleam that came from another world—her husband had said it so often that she knew it was there, even though she couldn't see it in the mirror. Sometimes she exploited it.

She arranged five chairs in a loose circle. If fewer people came, it wouldn't look empty, if it was more, the circle could be extended. She heard footsteps on the stairs. Her husband greeted her with a kiss, sat down in silence and closed his eyes. Jörg didn't join the circle but sat down by the wall, propped his arms on his knees and looked at the floor. His son and Dorle also avoided the free chairs in the circle, but pushed two chairs into a second row and looked expectantly at Karin. Ulrich and his wife sat on the empty chairs. "Is there a songbook?" Ulrich asked, and when Karin shook her head, he said, "Do you sing us something and then we sing it back?" Marko leaned against the wall next to Jörg and folded his arms, Ilse and Christiane brought chairs to the second row. Last came Margarete and Henner, who sat down a little apart from the others. With each new arrival Karin's heart grew heavier.

Karin sang three verses from the song about the golden sun—her husband and Ilse knew the words and joined in, a few of the others hummed the tune. Then she read out the line.

"That's the motto of Freiburg University," said Ulrich.

"That's the motto of the CIA," Marko added mockingly.

"It's the motto of all life," said Karin, and she talked about seeing and understanding. Who we are—if we see and understand, we have the chance to go beyond it. If not, we are trapped in it. For that reason, however, we mustn't impose the truth on others. Where truths are too painful and we are not a match for them, we all have our "life lies," the lies we need to keep on living, and what we must do is see and respect in others the truth of their pain as revealed by their life lies. But life lies do not only reveal pain, they also create it. Just as they stop us from seeing ourselves, they can also stop us from seeing others and letting ourselves be seen by them. Sometimes it is impossible without a struggle for truth, one's own and everyone else's.

"So you impose it," Andreas interjected.

"No, I'm talking about a struggle between equals, not one of force and compulsion."

Andreas wouldn't give in. "What about parents and children, husbands and financially dependent women, women and the men in love with them? Equals, or power and compulsion?"

Karin shook her head. "You get only one or the other. If you don't meet the other as equals, you may achieve power, but certainly not truth."

"If that's true, you can't impose truth on someone else. Why did you say we mustn't if we can't?"

Karin explained that she meant it's not just that you can't impose the truth, you shouldn't even try.

"But why shouldn't we be able to? Time and again in history truths have been imposed successfully—right truths as well as wrong ones."

Karin had got muddled. Does the interpretation of the line work only if truth is seen as the truth of the word of God? But she hadn't wanted to talk to her friends like that. Could she still go on talking like that? She had always seen the line as consistent in its worldly, analytic, therapeutic wisdom. She wanted to get to the conclusion, and end by saying that truth compelled was unblessed. But Andreas cited the German defeat in 1945 as a successful compulsion to truth, and she let it go. She smiled and said, "I don't know how to go on. I like the line—it gives me courage. But perhaps I don't understand it. Perhaps it isn't even true. Some people turn it around, so that it's not that the truth makes you free, it's that freedom makes things true. In that case there are as many truths as people freely living their lives—that idea scares me; I'd like there to be a single truth. But what does my wish count for! And what kind of prayer meeting was that! Thank you for coming and listening and let us say the Lord's Prayer."

Afterward Christiane organized breakfast: Ulrich went to the baker for rolls and took Jörg with him; Dorle and Ferdinand took care of grinding and brewing the coffee; Karin, her husband and Ilse sang hymns as they set the table and put out a plate of ham and a board of cheese; Andreas boiled the eggs and carefully packed them in a bed of towels; Margarete inspected the attic and the cellar with Henner. They were all glad to be active and not to have to talk.

Thirty-six

But how were they to escape talking? Only the perfectly happy escape it and the hopelessly despairing. As soon as the friends were sitting around the breakfast table, Jörg sat up in his chair and began.

"I know we were wrong and made mistakes. We took up a struggle that we could not win, so we should not have taken it up. We should have taken up a different struggle, not this one. We had to fight. Our parents conformed and shirked resistance—we couldn't repeat that. We couldn't simply watch children being burned by napalm in Vietnam, starving in Africa, being broken in institutions in Germany. Just as Benno Ohnesorg was shot, an attempt was made on Rudi Dutschke's life and a journalist who looked like him was almost lynched. While the state, with increasing impunity, showed its hideous mask of power, suppressing dissenters, the awkward, the unusable. While our comrades, before they were sentenced, before they could even stand before a court, were isolated, beaten, silenced. I know we misused violence. But resistance against a system of violence is impossible without violence."

Jörg had talked himself into a state of excitement. He had marshaled his speech so carefully that it sounded professorial at first, but he delivered it with growing confidence and passion. Most of them were squirming;

Jörg was talking the way people had thirty years ago and simply didn't anymore—it was embarrassing. His son, for whom the speech was particularly intended, struggled to seem bored and superior, and looked not at Jörg but at the wall or out of the window. Marko was wide-eyed with fascination; this was the Jörg he had been waiting for.

"I was rebuked for the attack on the American barracks, condemned too, of course, but rebuked by people like you. We couldn't put the bombs where the Americans committed their crimes, only where they prepared them and recovered from them. If one couldn't have attacked the SS in Auschwitz, one would have had to do it in Berlin, where they had prepared the extermination of the Jews, or in the Allgäu, where they had recovered from it. And as for the President—our lawyers fought for us to be seen and treated as prisoners of war and were unsuccessful, but he understood, he was with us in the war, he saw himself as a fighter, and us too."

Karin found the direction Jörg's speech was taking dangerous. "Let us . . ."

"I just want to say one more thing. I know I have been wrong and made mistakes. I don't expect you to approve of what I have done, or even think the state and society should have treated us more fairly. I just want the respect due to someone who has given everything for a larger cause and a good one, and who has paid for his errors and mistakes. Who has not sold himself, has asked for nothing and been given nothing. I never struck a deal with the other side, I never applied for special benefits, I never asked for mercy. I only made the applications anyone makes. We talked about it yesterday—I can't remember everything now, some things I've forgotten, but I've paid for it all." Jörg looked around the group. "So, that was what I wanted to say to you. Thank you for listening to me."

"If that's how you see it all—where did you actually go wrong, as you say, where did you make mistakes?" His son asked his question coldly and calmly.

"The victims. A struggle that doesn't lead to success doesn't justify victims."

"But if, with your actions, you had sparked the revolution in Germany or Europe or the world revolution, would the victims have been justified then?"

"Of course they would have been justified if we had created a better, fairer world through revolution."

"The sacrifice of innocent people?"

"The bad, unjust world we live in sacrifices innocent people too."

The son looked at his father, but said nothing more. He looked at him as if he were facing a monster with whom there could be no common ground.

"Do you really mean the sacrifice of innocent people is never justified?!" Jörg said. "If the only way to kill Hitler had involved innocent people . . ."

"That's an exception. You've turned the exception into the rule." Ferdinand turned to Eberhard, who was sitting next to him. "Would you pass me a roll, please?" He cut the roll open and beheaded an egg.

Jörg shook his head, but said nothing more. Eberhard passed the rolls, Christiane handed around the plate of ham and Margarete the cheese board. When

Dorle got up, picked up one coffeepot, went from seat to seat and poured, Ferdinand took the other one and did likewise. The conversation got under way, about the rain, the impending departure and journey home, the truth that makes you free and the freedom that makes things true, the changing times. Eberhard mentioned that, and although he didn't say so, everyone knew he was talking about Jörg's outmoded speech. "Even though they haven't been contradicted, the subjects, problems and theses of another era are simply finished. They sound wrong; anyone who represents them isolates himself, anyone who represents them passionately looks ridiculous. When I started my studies, all that counted was existentialism, at the end of my studies everyone was keen on analytic philosophy, and twenty years ago Kant and Hegel came back. The problems of existentialism hadn't been solved, nor had those of analytic philosophy. People were simply fed up with them."

Marko had listened attentively. "Because they haven't been solved, they come back. The RAF will come back too. Not as it was back then. But it will come back, and because capitalism has become global, it will fight capitalism globally too—more consistently than it did back then. The fact that it is no longer chic to speak of oppression, alienation and disenfranchisement doesn't mean they've gone away. In Asia young Muslims know what they have to fight against, and in Europe it's the young guys in the French suburbs, and in the flatlands of East Germany they don't know it yet, but they feel it. It's fermenting. If we all pull together . . ."

"Our terrorists saw themselves as part of our society. It was their society too; they wanted to change it
and thought it could be done only through violence.
The Muslims don't want to change our society, they
want to destroy it. You can forget your great coalition
of terrorists." Andreas asked mockingly, "Or is your
new RAF going to bomb its way to a theocratic state in
our country?"

Henner was lost in thoughts about his mother.
Sometimes she terrorized him with her demands, her
accusations, her complaining and nagging, her unerr-
ingly wounding remarks. She no longer played the
game where you're nice to others so that they will be
nice to you. It wasn't worth it for her anymore; why
should she be nice today so that others would be nice to
her tomorrow, when tomorrow she might be dead?
Were real terrorists like that? Had they stopped playing
according to the rules because they got nothing from
following them? Because, if poor, they had no chance of
success, and if rich, they experienced the game as men-
dacious, sordid, empty? He asked Margarete.

"Women know that. They play according to the
rules and achieve nothing, because the game is a men's
game and they're women. Some say to themselves that
in that case they won't commit themselves to the rules.
Others hope that, if they pay particularly faithful attention to the rules, they will one day be allowed to play on
an equal footing with the men."

"What about you?"

"Me? I've looked for a corner where I can play on

my own. But I understand the women who don't feel committed to the rules. I understand why so many of the terrorists were women."

"Could you . . ."

"You mean, if I didn't have my corner?" She laughed and took his hand. "I'd find myself another one!"

She pressed his hand and threw him a glance that drew his attention to Jörg. He was sitting opposite them. After his little speech he had said nothing more, hadn't eaten or drunk anything, had only stared straight ahead. He looked like someone who has done what had to be done, who is confident that it will have its effect, even if the effect will be a long time coming, who is at peace with himself, even if it isn't easy. He looked not happy, but contented. That suited the group as little as his speech suited the times, and for the first time Margarete was seized with sympathy. Jörg was locked in his perceptions and ideas. He carried his cell with him—presumably he had done so long before he was put in a cell—and she couldn't imagine how he would find his way out of it. She split a roll, put ham on one half and cheese on the other and set it on his plate. "Eat something, Jörg!"

His eyes returned to the table and found hers. He smiled. "Thank you."

"Your coffee's gone cold. I'll get you a fresh one."

"Oh, no. Cold coffee makes you handsome—don't you know that? It was often cold in prison."

"You're not in prison anymore. And you're handsome enough."

He smiled again, quite relaxed, grateful, trusting, as if she were tenderly spoiling him. "Yes, then thank you very much."

Margarete got up, picked up his cup, emptied it into the sink and waited as the water heated up and dripped through the filter. She heard the confusion of speaking, laughing voices at the breakfast table. Sometimes a loud word reached her: allotment, revolutionary somersault, damson cake, press declaration, and she wondered what they could be talking about. She was looking forward to the peace after the guests had left. Would Henner set off with the first or with the last or stay till evening? They had made no arrangements, no reunion out here, none in Berlin. For a whole night they had hugged each other and lain back to back and listened each to the other's breathing. They had listened to each other, but asked almost no questions. So little had happened between them and at the same time so much that Margarete could imagine anything. She was quite calm.

Thirty-seven

When she set the coffee down in front of Jörg, his thoughts were elsewhere. "Really too much," he said dismissively to Ulrich.

But Ulrich insisted they fetch Christiane's battery-powered radio and hear the broadcast of the President's speech. "Don't you remember how on New Year's Eve we always used to watch *Dinner for One* and then the President's speech? It was always a blast."

Andreas agreed. "You'll be asked about the speech. It's better that you know what's in it."

So the radio was fetched and switched on. The speaker explained that when the President had agreed to deliver this year's Berlin Cathedral speech, he had left the theme open. He wanted to talk about what people were preoccupied with at the time of the speech. Now the country knew, since a report in that morning's *Süddeutsche Zeitung* that the President had pardoned a terrorist on Friday, and that the terrorist had replied with a declaration of war. It was well known that the pardoning of terrorists had been an intense preoccupation of the President's over the past few months—it would come as no surprise if it was also the subject of the speech. At any rate leaving the subject open had been a brilliant idea on the part of the President or his spin doctor—the speaker stressed that the tension was great and the cathedral was full.

Jörg looked at Marko, aghast. "You've published the declaration? The one you showed me yesterday and I still wanted time to think about?"

"Yes. I had it legally checked—it can't do you any harm. Whether it matches your mood or meets your aesthetic demands or appeals to your sister—the revolution can't take that into account. So stand by it. The alternative is that you will make yourself look ridiculous." Marko, half serious, half joking, held his clenched fist aloft. "There's nothing in the declaration that you haven't said here this morning."

Jörg nodded wearily. Perhaps, he said to himself, Marko was right and the declaration was right and, as a consequence of what he had said that morning, necessary. But the right and the necessary can defeat you too. Everything had defeated him since he had been out of prison.

The speaker had faded at the end of a concluding chorale, followed by the bishop's greeting to the President. Then the President spoke.

He talked about terrorism in Germany from the seventies through the nineties, about the perpetrators and the victims, about the challenge to and preservation of the liberal state of law, about the obligation to respect and protect human dignity. This obligation made the state come down hard on those who attacked its citizens. But it also made it strong enough to remain measured in the defense of its order and, if no further danger existed, to end the struggle. The final goal was always the establishment of peace and reconciliation. There had been three terrorists still in prison. He had pardoned them all. He had wanted to give a sign that German terrorism and the tensions and fractures in society that it had provoked were past. We faced new threats, terrorist threats included, which we wanted to meet in a peaceful and reconciled state.

"I have dealt with and—as the media have reported—also met each individual. All three have put their pasts behind them. Putting the past behind one, if life consists only of that past and prison, isn't easy, and it isn't going to be easy for these three. Yesterday one of them issued a declaration, from which we shall read today. I see in it a man's attempt to put the past behind him, and at the same time to preserve it in his own biography. I regret the declaration. But I understand why someone without much time left to give his life a new meaning should make this desperate, contradictory attempt, just as he was torn between pleading for mercy and rebellious defiance."

The President paused briefly. People in the audience could be heard fidgeting, shifting, getting up and leaving. The President went on, turned to the relatives of the victims, acknowledged their desire for the whole truth and a sign of remorse or shame, and again deplored Jörg's declaration on their behalf. He thanked the congregation for allowing him to say what he had to say in the cathedral—it had been a good place for it.

The announcer informed the audience they had just heard the President, he had been giving this year's Berlin Cathedral speech, he had disclosed the pardoning of the last imprisoned terrorists. The announcer said there would shortly be a talk show about the President's speech and named the time and the participants: the daughter of a victim, a terrorist who had given himself up and been released long ago, a journalist who had made German terrorism the theme of his life, the minister of justice and the host. Then the announcer handed over to his colleagues in Wimbledon.

Thirty-eight

Ulrich turned the radio off. No one said anything. During the speech Jörg had pushed his chair back and first crossed his legs, then sat them side by side and propped his elbows on his knees and laid his head in his hands. Now he had to move, brought his chair to the table, tried to pour himself some coffee but couldn't do it. His hand was shaking. Christiane got to her feet, poured him a cup and put her other hand on his shoulder. "I asked him not to talk about it, and thought . . ." Jörg spoke quietly and as if he were close to tears.

Andreas said, "With your declaration you left him no other way out. How is the President to explain that he has pardoned a terrorist whose first act is to declare war on the state, if not like that? Is what he said true?"

"Of course not," Marko cut in. "The President just wanted to play down Jörg's declaration. Because they're afraid of Jörg, they turn him into a helpless, contradictory joke figure. But the comrades understand what's going on here, and it really couldn't have gone any better . . ."

"Stop your stupid chattering. Is it true, Jörg?"

"I . . ."

"Stop your idiotic interrogation," said Christiane. "You aren't his friend, as I thought, you're just his lawyer, and . . ."

"Leave it, Christiane. Yes, I don't have much time left. I've got cancer, discovered too late, bad operation, bad radiation therapy, or else so late that there was nothing to be done, and now I've got metastases."

"Why didn't I know anything about that?" Christiane replied.

Jörg laughed contemptuously. "Prostate cancer. I can't get it up anymore, I can't keep my water in—am I supposed to tell a woman about that? Yes, you're my sister, but . . ." He made a face and shook his head. "OK, Dorle? You couldn't have chosen a worse one. I didn't want to tell you—now everyone knows. What else do you want to know? Whether I was, as he put it, 'torn between pleading for mercy and rebellious defiance'? Yes, I was. I wanted to live again before the cancer devoured me, even if there wasn't much left of my life. Smelling the forest and the wet dust when it rains in the city after a run of hot days, driving on little French country roads with the sunroof and the windows open, going to the cinema, eating pasta and drinking red wine with friends." He smiled with resignation at the others. "I hadn't imagined it would be so difficult. And Marko seduced me into thinking I could play a part again and everything I had done, outside and in, would not be for nothing. I'm not accusing you of anything, Marko— you didn't put the idea into my head; I thought it myself. In my request for a pardon I still showed restraint. When I had my conversation with the President . . . I'd just had the diagnosis with the metastases, and he said, It'll go no further, and then out it came. I should have been killed in a shootout twenty-five years ago."

Christiane was still standing next to him, her hand on his shoulder. "To make sure that didn't happen, I betrayed you back then. I couldn't stand feeling so anxious about you. I thought, I didn't bring you up to be shot by the police. And one day you will even be happy still to be alive. And now if you aren't—I'm sorry. I'm sorry about everything, about betraying you back then, and about the fact that I'd do it again, and that you have cancer and don't want to live anymore and that this weekend has become so difficult." She was crying.

Karin wanted to stand up, but her husband held her tight. It was quiet in the room; the rain rustled outside. Jörg looked up. The tears ran down his sister's face and dripped from her chin to the floor. Her shoulders shook—everything was terrible, everything was hopeless. He put his head on her hand.

When he got up again, he asked Ulrich, "Does your offer still hold? Can I start in one of your labs?"

"Whenever you like."

"Where are your labs?"

"Hamburg, Berlin, Cologne, Karlsruhe, Heidelberg—you remember the pub where we used to play cards, before you abandoned such profane things? That's one of my labs now too."

"You see, I'd even forgotten that I used to play cards. But I like going back to where it all began. I can't go under your wing, Tia. I wouldn't do you any good, or you me. Visiting and holidays, that's different. But in the same flat, over breakfast at the kitchen table in the morning, in the evening on the sofa in front of the television, my diapers in the bathroom—we can't have that."

Christiane nodded. She was too relieved to be able to contradict him. She sniffed, wiped away her tears and started clearing away the plates and cutlery.

"Sit down." Margarete rested her hand on her arm, and Christiane sat down. "The cellar is full of water. It'll have to be bailed out, and I'd be happy if you could all help me. The fire department has its hands full with schools and hospitals and government offices—we know that already. I think the rain will stop in an hour—shall we meet then?"

The sky was as gloomy and the rain as steady as it had been in the morning and the evening before. Ulrich, who wanted to know everything, wanted to know that too. "Of course we'll help, but what makes you think the rain's about to stop?"

"You hear the birds? They start when the rain's about to stop. I don't know why, but that's how it is."

They listened to the sounds outside, and amid the rustle of the rain they heard the singing and twittering and chattering of the birds.

Thirty-nine

When the plates and cutlery had been cleared away and washed, Jörg went in search of his son. He didn't find him in the house, and when he asked Margarete if there was a place in the garden sheltered from the rain, she told him how to get to the greenhouse. It was broken and should have been torn down, but part of the glass roof was still intact, and she sometimes sat under it in the rain on an overturned bathtub.

Margarete was right—the rain was easing off. But Jörg had forgotten the directions she had given him as soon as she had finished speaking. He went on searching and was soaked by the time he reached the greenhouse and finally found his son. He sat down silently next to him and was glad for the time being that his son didn't get up and go. He shivered, and he would have liked to warm himself up by beating his chest and sides with his arms. But he didn't want to risk repelling his son and driving him away. So he sat still and saw the rain getting weaker and weaker. Then he said: "I really did write you lots of letters."

Ferdinand took his time. "I can ask my grandparents for the letters." He spoke as if it were nothing.

Once again Jörg took a long time before he spoke the next sentence. "I know I hurt you and your mother." He waited for a reaction. When none came, he went on. "Asking forgiveness—it's such a small request, just a few words, and what happened is so difficult. I can't bring it all together. So I don't dare."

Ferdinand looked briefly at his father. As quickly as he examined him he condemned him. "Have you already forgotten what you said last night and this morning? You have no reason to regret Mother any more than your other victims. Certainly not me—I'm still alive."

He said that so defensively that Jörg was once again afraid his son would stand up and go. He tried to think of something cautious to say next.

But his son was quicker. "Don't imagine I'm sympathetic to you because you have cancer and wear diapers. I couldn't care less."

Could they see each other again, Jörg had wanted to ask his son. But he didn't dare. "Can I write to you? Will you give me your address? Christiane only has the one for your grandparents."

Ferdinand asked defensively back: "What do you want from me?"

Jörg had the feeling that everything else depended on the answer to this question. What was he supposed to say? Why, before, when he had talked about the things of life, had he not talked about his son? He hadn't thought about him. He had got used to not thinking about him in jail. He said, "I'd like to be able to think about you again."

"If you didn't find time to do that in jail, you certainly won't find it in freedom." Ferdinand got up and went.

"I . . ." But Jörg didn't call after his son that it wasn't a matter of time. Ferdinand couldn't really mean that. Jörg watched him go, found him as awkward in his movements as he himself felt when he moved and knew he was being observed or when he observed himself. His son's defensiveness, sharpness, brusqueness he also knew from himself. That made his heart soft and heavy. Yes, this young man was his son. Yes, he was vulnerable as he himself had been vulnerable. Even growing up without a mother was something he had passed on to him.

The rain had stopped. Jörg looked at the clock. Before his assignment in the cellar he still had time to pack his things. Someone would take him to Berlin, then he would sit in the train, find a room tomorrow and start work in the lab on Tuesday. Perhaps he would even like the work, but at least he would like the people who would leave him in peace and accept him if he did good work.

On the way back to the house he met Margarete and Henner. "You see," she said, looked to the sky and spread her arms wide.

"I see," he laughed. "I see."

"He actually laughed," Margarete said to Henner as they walked on.

"I think that if you become a terrorist and kill people, you have to be quite a tough character."

"Are you a tough character?"

"If you become a journalist and report on how people kill one another, you have to . . . I don't know, Margarete. And I don't know whether I should stay a journalist. I don't know what'll happen with my mother. I don't know what'll happen with women. I don't know much this morning."

"The bench is wet—I could have thought of that and brought a towel."

Henner sat down. "Sit on my lap!"

Margarete blushed. "You're insane."

"No," he said and laughed cheerfully at her. "I'm not insane. I want to have you on my lap."

"But the bench . . ."

He clapped his hands invitingly on his legs. She sat down carefully. "You see," he said, and put his arms around her. Again he felt as if he were holding a tree or a rock and as if at last nothing could blow him away. Her heaviness held him tight, kept him rooted. When Margarete abandoned her reserve, softened in his arms, pressed herself to him and laid her face in the well of his neck, she asked, "Are you still all right? Am I too heavy?" He shook his head.

She went to sleep in his arms and woke up in his arms. "Do we have to go?"

"You slept for only a few minutes—we still have a bit of time. Would you . . . do you think you could . . ." Now Henner blushed.

"What?"

"Will you have me on your lap for a moment?"

She laughed and stood up. "Come on, then!" She sat down and pulled him onto her lap. He couldn't cuddle up as he would have liked to. Was he too big for her? Was he too heavy for her? Did she despise his childlike need to be sat on her lap? He sighed.

She whispered in his ear: "Everything's fine."

He let himself go, big, but not too big, heavy, but not too heavy, and his need to be sat on her lap was the most natural need in the world to her. Everything really was fine.

"How much time do we have?"

"None. Will we see each other again?"

"Yes."

"Good." Henner jumped up, stretched a hand out to Margarete and pulled her to her feet.

Forty

They all turned up. The two couples arrived together; they had met by the cars as they loaded in their things. Would they see one another again, in Salzburg or Bayreuth? Andreas and Marko stood and argued until Jörg joined them and said he didn't want any complaints about the press declaration that had been published without his authorization. It had happened, it was over. Ilse asked Christiane whether she could rent a room to write during her next holidays. Dorle stood next to Ferdinand, said something into his ear, stroked his arm, his back, ran her hand over his cheek, and he liked that, and at the same time it was embarrassing, because he wanted to appear implacable in front of his father. They were all ready to set off.

Margarete looked from one to the other. "The water is calf-deep. At the very least you should take off your shoes and socks and roll your trousers up over your knees. It's dirty and it will splash—haven't you got anything worse to put on? Dorle? Your T-shirt won't be pink afterward."

But they all let it go at bare feet and rolled-up trousers. They stuck their socks in their shoes and put their shoes side by side—lined up like the taxis outside the opera house. Margarete arranged the friends in a row from the cellar up the steps to the garden and back to the cellar window. "Every ten minutes we'll move on so that we don't get bored. I have only seven buckets; so there will always be a moment to pause for breath."

Marko filled the first bucket and passed it to Andreas at the bottom of the steps. Via Ilse, Jörg and Ingeborg the bucket wandered up the steps, was passed on from Ferdinand to Margarete, from her to Ulrich and from him to Karin, who poured it into the field next to Margarete's garden house and gave it to Henner, who threw it to Dorle, from whom it was passed to Christiane, who dropped it through the cellar window to Eberhard, who gave it to Marko.

Marko handed Andreas the bucket with such brio that a little water always slopped over the edge and splashed him. Jörg meant well, bent lower to Ilse and stretched higher to Ingeborg than necessary and was soon drenched in sweat. Ferdinand, Margarete and Ulrich stood in the sun that had pierced the clouds, and joked gleefully with Henner, Dorle and Christiane. Full-bucket thoroughbreds versus empty-bucket softies, Stakhanovites versus freeloaders, water carriers versus water throwers, no, bucket throwers. Karin poured out the bucket with a sweeping, benedictory gesture. When, after the twelfth shift of positions, it was Marko's turn to stand under the window and Andreas's turn to bail, Marko tried to do the same thing to Andreas again. But Andreas kept his guard up. By then the water level had fallen anyway, the bucket wouldn't fill, and Margarete shortened the line and sent Christiane and Eberhard downstairs with brooms to sweep the water from the back part to the front.

They were all preoccupied with their buckets or brooms, with their wet feet and damp clothes, with their neighbor or their opposite number, with themselves. Only Ilse looked at the others: Marko and Andreas at odds with each other, Dorle and Ferdinand hesitating about whether or not to fall in love and Margarete and Henner quite ready to do so, the two married couples safe in the self-evident state of belonging together, Christiane relieved that the bombs had either been defused or had exploded without doing any great damage, Jörg happy that he didn't have to master anything but buckets and water. Ilse looked at the individuals and was fascinated by the whole, by the spectacle of collaboration, by the coordination of bodies and hands, by the dissolution of the individuals, with their sympathies and antipathies, into a common task. Would she let Jan experience anything like that? Was the joint planning and execution of terrorist attacks similar in nature? Or was it, when attacks were being planned, more a matter of coordinating autonomous, independent acts?

As easily as the friends had formed themselves into a whole, they would also fall apart again. Nothing, she thought sadly, would remain of the whole. Then she laughed. The cellar! The cellar was dry.

They sat around the table on the terrace for the last time. Exhausted, cheerful, only half of them there, the other half already en route or already home. It occurred to Ulrich that he could hand around a sheet of paper on which each of them would write their phone number and e-mail address, and pass the list on to everyone. But he didn't. Karin didn't deliver a travel blessing, Christiane spoke no words of farewell and Jörg gave no thanks for being welcomed into freedom. They drank water and didn't speak much. They looked into the park. A strong wind had blown away the clouds, the sky was a radiant blue and trees, bushes and house glittered fresh with rain. Then everyone left at the same time. Karin and her husband took Ilse and Jörg with them to Berlin. Ferdinand preferred to be driven by Marko. But he gave Christiane a piece of paper with his address and telephone number; if she wanted, she could give it to his father as well. Christiane and Margarete stood at the gate and waved until they could no longer see the cars.

A NOTE ABOUT THE TRANSLATOR

Shaun Whiteside's translations from German include works by Freud, Nietzsche, Schnitzler and Musil. His translation of *Magdalene the Sinner* by Lilian Faschinger was awarded the Schlegel-Tieck Prize in 1997.